WITHOUT
SAYING
GOODBYE

WITHOUT SAYING GOODBYE

Maryam Sachs

Translated by
SARA SUGIHARA

QUARTET

First published in 2009 by
Quartet Books Limited
A member of the Namara Group
27 Goodge Street, London W1T 2LD

Copyright © Maryam Sachs 2009
Translation copyright © Sara Sugihara 2009

The right of Maryam Sachs to be identified
as the author of this work has been asserted
by her in accordance with the
Copyright, Designs and Patents Act, 1988

All rights reserved.
No part of this book may be reproduced in
any form or by any means without prior
written permission from the publisher

A catalogue record for this book
is available from the British Library

ISBN   978 0 7043 7178 1

Typeset by Antony Gray
Printed and bound in Great Britain by
T J International Ltd, Padstow, Cornwall

TO
JOUNAM

ACKNOWLEDGEMENTS

All my thanks to Naim Attallah whose energy, sensitivity and brilliant decisiveness brought this book to light in England. My sincerest thanks to Sara Sugihara for her creative mind in translating while feeling the emotions. My special thanks to Anna Stothard for her refined and delicate work with words, shaping the best translation I could imagine.

I survived my desires
And left behind my dreams. Lucid,
I can only suffer,
Facing the fruit of my empty heart.

Pushkin

DAY ONE

It is the stars,
The stars above us, govern our conditions.

Shakespeare, *King Lear*, iv, 3

I NEVER wanted to learn to drive. I can walk for a long time, for a very long time. And I run until breathless, absolutely parched. While running, I am laying down lifelines, plans for my survival. I leave footprints in all the countries of the world – except my own, for I am an exile. Sometimes I take buses, trams and taxis, but I'll walk if it is too early or too late to catch the Métro. Night or day I wander through the city, feeding on its secrets as if I were about to depart on a trip, my soul as my only baggage.

I can do that and more, but I do not drive. I cannot. The attention, the concentration required, would distract me from the tiny celestial signs that make an ordinary life into a story, a real story, filled with characters and encounters, forbidden places and heroic battles. The steps taken one night, supposedly at random and without direction, can turn into life's most bittersweet treasures. Walking is a way to keep alive the mystery of my destiny, as one might blow softly on a flickering candle flame, like the tuberose-scented taper always burning somewhere in my house: a mystical, voluptuous memory of my lost country. I love to listen to the little voice which accompanies my steps, the murmured: 'What if?' As in, what if I had not gone into that bar? What if we had not seen each other at the restaurant?

To understand a city, writes the Iranian philosopher Dariush Shayegun, is to accept three sensations that mingle there: the forbidden, the tempting, and the beautiful. 'You don't want to grow up because you refuse to become autonomous,' says my husband Kamran, who sometimes sees me only as the spoiled little Iranian exile who said 'yes' to him fourteen years ago, one March 21st, the first day of spring. In Iran, that day is celebrated as our New Year's Day and is traditionally a lucky day to marry. I answer: 'No, you're wrong, I'm making progress. When you travel to the other side of the world on business, I no longer have to run home to my parents, I no longer ask you how long you'll be away, whom you'll be seeing, and in which hotel you'll be staying.'

'Madame?'

Yes, I walk, or I let someone drive me . . .

'Madame!'

I jump, as the taxi-driver looks accusingly at me. I am caught, and guilty, too, because everything I had hoped to avoid is happening right now, silently, in the back of this taxi, on this vinyl back-seat where I should be sitting alone, going home to wait for my husband to call from Madrid. I am even supposed to be joining him there in a couple of days.

I look at my hands, covered with blood, and *his* hands, the other passenger's, this fine spring night: thin, bony, with nearly transparent skin. They too are stained with blood. I press my silk scarf to his wound, wanting the softest of bandages for him, the finest veil, like a caress he might remember when he awakens. I am holding his wan face, with its closed eyes, in the crook of my arm. I have the overwhelming sensation of rocking a child and can think of only one thing: I must protect him. Like nearly all Middle Eastern women, I was born mother and daughter at the same time, a child yet also a woman. I want somehow to warm him, but do not know how. Perhaps he is not even cold. He is barely breathing. I let my eyes wander over his thick lashes, his straight nose, the precise oval of his face, his mouth, and the slight line of bitterness there . . . I feel so close to this man I do not know. One of my long, dark locks of hair is brushing his ear, light as a feather. I sit up a bit and manage to pull my hair back with one hand, afraid even the slightest movement may disturb his sleep. What should I do? The taxi continues along the quai Branly, and then slows down a little, the driver turning towards me, looking distrustfully at me. I can see that this is his last fare, and that he wants to go home.

'Madame, am I taking you to the hospital?'

The hospital, of course.

'Yes, take us to the nearest hospital.'

'We don't have a choice. This young man is in trouble, he needs to be examined immediately . . . '

'Yes, yes, you're right,' I murmur.

A wave of images streams through my head. Questions, too . . . Why didn't I call the police or an ambulance instead of trying to play the heroine? Did I really need to throw away my life, the life I share with Kamran, to burst headlong into someone else's? The taxi driver turns the radio on and accelerates slightly, ignoring the rain, which has been falling for hours. I hear, as if in a dream, news of my own country, a place I have not seen since 1979. I think of my parents. My mother stepped into her new life, with exemplary strength and courage, for me, her only daughter, so that I would be able to live a normal life and go to a good school, so that I would be able to marry, to have a family. She rebuilt, redecorated, made new friends, discovered new landmarks, and tamped down her feelings of nostalgia. She taught me that our thoughts, our souls and our childhood memories were the only baggage an exile needs when far from her country. With these riches inside of me I would be able to cross any border and never feel lonely or uprooted. She taught me that during moments of pain and suffering, all material things disappear from the sphere of our concern, becoming worthless in the face of the essence of our existence: love, tenderness, altruism, and the unconditional bonds of family. She told me that an incredible strength lies deep inside us for when we need it. My mother showed me that cities are like clay and that each person inside that city, permanently or not, is a potential sculptor of that clay. If they are patient, one day they will go beyond the transitory to make their home there. Like a genius of Iranian architecture, they will use the light as if it were the centre, the pit of each fruit, creating both an exterior and an interior life. For my father, leaving was the final farewell to our country. He suffered, and his suffering moves me. I know that he will never forget what he had to leave behind: our house in Tehran, its Eden-like gardens full of waterfalls and cool streams, the dizzying fragrance of jasmine, the birds singing . . . even the dust.

The sadly banal newsflash about my home country is followed by music from a film soundtrack. A few piano chords cover the back-and-forth monotony of the windscreen wipers. The music is soft and my passenger is unconscious, artificially asleep thanks to a reckless driver and his swerving car, yet I still want to warn the taxi driver not to wake our passenger with the radio music. If he wakes up, he is going to feel pain, and I do not want him to feel pain. I know the melody from the radio, I can even hum it to myself, but I cannot quite identify these melancholy chords. Images come flooding into my head, the faces of the actors in the film – and then I remember, it's from *Les Choses de la Vie* (These Things Happen), yes, that's it, the score from *Les Choses de la Vie*. I don't remember who directed it. I know it was a Frenchman, but I can only see the handsome, tormented faces of Romy Schneider and Michel Piccoli. A man, a woman, destiny . . . perhaps something similar to what I am experiencing at this very moment. I wouldn't give this up; there is no way I would trust someone else to take my unknown man towards the place of his resurrection and of my hope. Right now he is mine. In a few minutes he will be in the hands of paramedics, doctors and nurses, who will try to diagnose what is wrong with him. Other faces will be scrutinising him, bending over him. And tomorrow – although it is almost tomorrow now – his family will come to look after him. I see no ring on his finger, but that doesn't mean anything.

Blue, yellow, black, or green; French, American, English, or Mexican, the world's taxis keep our secrets and our lies hidden from view. Like mirrors in hotel rooms, they've seen it all, heard it all, recorded it all: the complaints, the tears, the giggles, the fights over the background music or the insipid political commentary. They are the indiscreet witnesses of our past, our present and our future, and no one escapes them. No one. The taxi rolls on and I know it will be stopping soon, the hospital is only a few metres away. I sit up a little on the seat, trying to avoid any sudden movement. When I see the 'Accident and Emergency' sign I know it'll be too late to decide. *Decide*. The word sounds so strange.

The crash only took a second. I heard a brief, agitated cry, and I remember a car speeding away so quickly in the night that it was impossible to see the make, the colour, or the first few numbers on the licence plate. Then I run towards the victim as he falls, like a wounded bird, on to the asphalt. I see his blood and don't know what to do. The quai Malaquais is deserted. A little farther along, but too far for me to risk stepping away from the victim, I see the lights of a *bar tabac,* its great iron shutter lowering. It is Sunday night and I have just had dinner with a couple of friends in a brasserie in the neighbourhood. I kneel next to the unknown man, feeling so happy and yet so miserable at the same time. An inexplicable possessiveness is guiding me, speaking to me. There are times we find ourselves able to do anything: *the forbidden, the tempting, the beautiful* . . . He will not, *he cannot*, die in my arms. Not like this. Not now. I find myself murmuring a few lines from the Koran: 'Nothing can touch you beyond that which God has planned for you . . . ' I am crying and shaking at the same time. I search for a piece of paper, an ID of some kind for this unknown man who is no longer so unknown, who will no longer be unknown to me, daring to slide my hand into one of the pockets of his beige raincoat. No iPod, no diary, no address book which might give me a clue as to his identity. Feverishly I reach into his other pocket and find a laminated ID card and a thin book. On the card is written *Sergei Krasin*, student at the Sorbonne. So his name is Sergei. A Russian name. Is he an exile, too? I have a better understanding of his big pale eyes, his wheat-blond hair, the slight disillusionment that I noticed in his smile at the restaurant, where our eyes met for the first time. The book is a collection of love poems by Pablo Neruda, in the original Spanish. A Russian who reads Spanish? The sound of car brakes startles me, a taxi is stopping near us. Quickly I put back the ID and the book. My personal countdown to guilt has begun. What am I doing here? I should be at home in my bed with a good book, or worse, stuck watching a film-of-the-week on television. Too late.

Too late – or maybe too early? The driver rolls down his window: 'Madame, do you need help?' he says.

And now: 'Madame, we're here. A & E is just over there . . . '

I emerge from my thoughts. I cannot let the driver go any further, or ask any questions I don't want to have to answer. What? You don't know this man? If he is not your husband, your brother, not a friend or a lover, then who is he? No, the driver must not ask me anything. I untangle myself slowly, as I might from a child to whom I have just told a bedtime story, and with my left hand I grab the door handle. I am going to get out of the car and run away, far away in the night, like a thief, stammering: 'Please, take care of him . . . '

The driver turns towards me. I am looking down, hiding my face in the collar of my raincoat, my hair fanned out to cover me. It is dark outside, and dark in the car. 'She had long hair and wore a navy-blue raincoat,' that's what he'd tell the sketch artist if they asked him. He would not remember the silk scarf, men rarely remember those kind of details.

'What d'you mean take care of him? Are you telling me you don't know this man?'

'Er . . . yes, but . . . listen . . . please don't mention me, tell them you found him. Please make sure he's all right, OK?'

'Madame, wait!'

I get out of the car. And I run. I run, fly, as fast as I

did when I was a student at UC Berkeley in California, when they called me the 'jogging queen'. I never missed that *rendezvous* with myself, that wonderful time of solitude. There was a joy in the miles I covered, my headphones on, listening to my heart beat, to music I chose fresh each morning. Sad, sick – I would not give up that tête-à-tête with my moods and my secret emotions, before going back to the turmoil of the world, and the pursuit of learning.

I don't think, I run. My high heels don't even slow me down. If I trip and fall, too bad, but I know it won't happen. There is only room for one injured person in this story. It is mathematically impossible for me to fall, since what then would be my function? I have always had a function, something to do for someone else – that is my vocation, my destiny as a Middle Eastern woman, the deepest part of me.

And suddenly I find my way, past the antique shops, a couple of small art galleries, a few familiar-looking lamp-posts. I know this neighbourhood as if I'd been born here, recognising each building's façade, each café and bus stop. I have always lived in the 7th *arrondissement*, I have also worked in this area for years, and now all of a sudden I have a new neighbour. A Russian. His name is Sergei, he has eyes as blue as the sky and he lives at 14, rue Jacob, which I read on his student ID. We are separated by a few streets, but it is insignificant for those who travel as much as we do. Is he married? Does he have children? Does he still have family in Russia, and why did he leave his country? And his flat? What does it look like? Small, modestly furnished? Probably, since he is a student. Unless he works somewhere to pay for his studies? No, he must live in a 'chambre de bonne' or share a flat like I did in Berkeley. My God, what am I doing? It is after one o'clock in the morning. My husband is probably worried by now, he will have left dozens of messages on our answering machine, since I don't have a mobile phone. 'Roxane, you need a mobile,' is what Kamran says to me every day, 'everyone has one these days, except you'. He adds, chuckling – he is really not a jealous man: 'Otherwise I am going to think you're hiding things from me.' I like that 'except you', those two little words remind me how even as a child I needed to defy the established rules, and that my need to be contrary is firmly rooted. Also, even though I do speak French correctly, I have always had trouble with certain sounds, so I might hear 'accept you' instead of 'except you'. Kamran is right to think of me this way, as though I were an inexperienced or stubborn child, or both together. I do not want to learn to drive; I don't want a computer or a mobile. Is this why I decided to save this man and then immediately abandon him? It makes no sense. And yet – I know how passion grows in the space between good and evil, between joy and pain. I desire him and I suffer because of that desire. Tomorrow. 'Tomorrow is a new day and a fresh start,' say the Iranians. Tomorrow, at first light, I will figure out how to get to the hospital.

I will make up an excuse for arriving late at the bookshop on the boulevard Raspail where I work. I will say I am sick, that I slipped on the street . . . it was raining, I was wearing high heels . . . I know how to twist the truth, even if I hate lying. I do not work with books for nothing. Should I go to the nearest police station? Ask around his building? No, the hospital, that's better. I will sneak through the halls, push open the door to his room, approach his bed. I will watch over him in silence, my eyes telling him what my lips never will: 'My angel, tonight I saved you.'

I imagine my life as a painting. It is a painting on which I highlight the unforgettable moments, adding layers of colour to its tinted background. Destiny also appears on the canvases of life: shining, creating, repeating, and eventually tarnishing. Some paintings are more colourful than others. It all depends on the imaginative power of the individual who paints it. We all try to draw masterfully on our canvases, but sometimes the moment escapes us and it is then that the challenge begins. From the age of twelve, I painted my future husband on the canvas of my life.

My grandmother was married at the age of fifteen, my mother at seventeen, and I was married at twenty-one. They were not allowed to choose their husbands, but I did. I was twelve and he was the son of a friend of my parents. One look from him and I gave in, swayed by the delicious power of his honeyed eyes, his black hair, his strength. Kamran lived in Ashtian, I lived in Tehran. Our families frequently dined together, so there would have been a large group of us enjoying ourselves in the magnificent gardens near our house. It was a summer night, the air was scented with jasmine and *shabgol*, a rare flower that opens only after dusk. The legend says that it awakens the senses of all those who breathe in its scent. It is a flower which opens for lovers' meetings, a sensitive flower which responds to great feeling and passion. I don't know if I noticed its magical scent that night, but I do know that my adolescent eyes saw in Kamran the man who would be their absolute master. He was ten years older than me, but in Iran the age difference is not as important as it is in Western countries. My mother married a man fifteen years her senior, and her love for him never faltered through the difficult years.

Kamran had a beautiful soul. His distinctive physique and his charisma attracted flocks of young women, all of whom adored him and would do anything for him. Of course they hated me on sight. They understood, perhaps even before I did, that we were made for each other, for better and for worse. Kamran lost his father when he was only a child, and he had been the head of his family since then. He carried that responsibility like a second skin. His generosity of spirit made him even more handsome, more radiant, and I wanted to be a source of light for him, so that he would see and desire only me, so he would forget the innocence of my twelve years.

Under the starry sky of an Iranian night, we both stepped into the painting which I had been secretly painting since I was old enough to follow my dreams. We were already written in the literature of destiny: Roxane and Kamran. For ever. After we met that first time, he waited while I grew up a bit. My parents wanted me to study in Europe, then in the United States. My mother wanted me to have a good education, my father wanted me to have 'book learning' so that I might one day become independent. They taught me the value of work, and the joy of being autonomous. Their openness allowed me to escape being submerged into the classic matrimonial pattern of my country. I was allowed to exist, to love, and be loved, and most of all I was given respect.

Kamran, whose ideas followed those of my parents, worked with great determination, planning for a career in publishing. Finally he asked my family for my hand. There was no opposition to our union. On the contrary, the revolution had brought us closer together. We were living in the same situation, experiencing the same pain in exile, the same dream of inventing a new life abroad.

I was married far from my country. The first day of spring. A new season, a new life. In Iran, this important date symbolises hope, new growth in the fields, the awakening of nature, the smiles of children. Each Iranian puts on new clothing, bought specially for the day. Flowers, candles, fruits, fish, sweets . . . according to tradition, all the symbols of happiness, wealth, prosperity, health, *joie de vivre* and fertility must be represented. I remember . . . You and I, at my parents' house in Paris, and, as is the custom, we are both sitting on a small bench, facing a mirror which is lit by candelabra. I am wearing an ivory-coloured dress, embroidered with tiny pearls, custom-sewn by one of my cousins, who is a talented seamstress. Around my neck, my wrists, and on my ears, I am wearing our family jewels, in heavy yellow gold, with jewels only the master goldsmiths of Yazd know how to create. On either side of me, two married women are holding a large white veil at arm's length, while other women walk behind us rubbing two sugar cones together, creating a mist of sugary grains which foretells happiness. At the same time, a *mullah* recites verses of the Koran that speak of the institution of marriage, the sacred and indestructible bonds which will unite us from now on. In my country, divorce is rare, and when it happens, only the husband may request it. 'Will you take this man . . . ' I do not know if it is the first, the second, or the third time I am asked this question in Persian. I know only that a young Iranian girl is not supposed to answer too quickly, she is supposed to maintain the suspense. The husband is supposed to speak first, and right away. I saw Kamran's 'yes' reflected in the mirror, a symbol of clarity and transparency, his lips opening to form the sacred words. So I wait, and I wait some more. The impatience rising in me tells me I must begin, that this is the beginning. In a quivering voice I say, '*Balé*, yes, I will take you, Kamran, for my husband.'

The silence is broken, waves of euphoria wash over us. The flashbulbs spark, immortalising the intense pleasure of the moment. The kisses and elated voices seem to flow down from the sky.

Under the dynasty of the Kadjars, in another time, a young girl of fifteen was also preparing to marry her Prince Charming. My grandmother married Prince Muhammad Hassan Mirza. He was her first man, and she was his fifth and last wife . . . He nicknamed her *Sogoli*, meaning 'the favourite'. Like all the other men who had asked for her hand, he was won over by her porcelain complexion, her emerald green eyes, her grace, her candour, her passionate nature; the Persian and Turkish blood flowing through her veins. The prince was the man that my grandmother's father chose for the daughter he called *the apple of his eye,* worthy of a prince's ring. At the time, the royal family was living in indescribable luxury and pleasure. There was an unending, frenetic series of feasts, hunting parties and polo games, all at considerable and extravagant expense to the state, which was already reeling, close to bankruptcy. My grandmother became at once a woman, a princess, and mother to a male child. She accepted her responsibilities with sincerity and dignity. Unfortunately the political climate continued to deteriorate. After the *coup d'état*, Reza Shah dethroned the Kadjars and ordered the royal family into exile. The prince, deprived of his *Sogoli*, left Iran, his heart broken, taking with him their young son.

My grandmother's parents decided their daughter was too young to set out on such an adventure, and they kept her with them, thinking already of marrying her again, in spite of the desperate love letters the young woman was receiving from her beloved prince and her dear son, the fruit of an impossible love.

When Reza Shah came to power, women gained autonomy and independence, and the wearing of the *chador* was forbidden. Modelling his regime upon that of Kemal Atatürk, Reza Shah laid out his vision of a Westernised society. However, traditional families were frightened, refusing to accept the changes. Iran wanted to display its will to change, its movement towards a more open way of life. And my grandmother, pushed somewhat by her parents, remarried . . . Fifty years later, her life was shattered again by the Islamic revolution and she was devastated as she watched her children leaving the country. Perhaps the revolutions empowered women and increased their maternal instincts, but emotional scars remained, and can never be erased.

Yes, I saw my life as a painting. My grandmother and my mother had this dream before I did. They chose the same colours: blood red, the symbol of life and of love; blue, for hope; white for purity; and ochre, orange and beige, the colours of the earth, to symbolise the pain of their exile. Three generations of women, each feeling the pain of the same leave-takings without a farewell.

Kamran and I, over the years, spoke more and more often of the past, but the discussion almost always veered towards feelings of regret, of sadness and disappointment. These immobile forays, sometimes silent, sometimes chatty, reassured us, as we owed our survival to the memories of our lost childhoods. We share the same passion for books – he edits them and I sell them – we love the same writers, Zweig, Turgenev, Miller; their wounds are like ours. 'This is how I can be at home nowhere: I am a stranger everywhere, a guest in the best of all worlds,' writes Stefan Zweig.

But sometimes we didn't understand each other, our wounded hearts travelling different paths, each of us tending to and bandaging our own wounds, and the true background of the painting we were dreaming about became nostalgia. And there was the baby we so desired, which still had not yet come. There too, hope faltered. During the difficult moments, I berated myself: 'You're a sterile exile,' and this incredibly negative, cruel thought terrified me. And the colour black began to creep across my painting.

Kamran fled. He buried himself in his work, travelling, the jammed diary of the busy man. Our marriage had been derailed without us realising. And when my friends would see me standing alone – in my melancholy – at one of those opening-night cocktail parties, those endless evenings, they would whisper, 'Your husband must be the Invisible Man, we never see you together!' I would defend him, explaining his obligations, how much he had to travel.

I spoke to my mother, my friend, my confidante, my

most faithful adviser. I told her I was afraid the fire might be dying down, the bloom of our passion withering, its petals falling . . . Would it not be better to abstain from loving him now, in order to avoid the pain of losing him in the future? I wanted her to tell me again the story of my grandmother and her prince. She replied: 'My dear, you have married well. This may be a difficult time right now but it will all work out as soon as you have a child. At your age, you still have so many chances, you must not lose hope. Besides, Kamran is such a good man.' Yes, he was, good, gentle . . . *But where do you put love when you take it out of its perfect jewel box?* I had been asking myself this more and more often. But I did not find the answer. I loved Kamran from the bottom of my heart. I admired him, seeing him still through the eyes of a twelve-year-old girl. I am grateful for everything he has done and continues to do for me, rendering my exile less painful by giving me a balanced and comfortable life, but we were like a surviving brother and sister trying to rebuild that which they had lost. To stop halfway would be a terrible mistake. But. You only need one thing to bring two souls together. Or to separate them for ever. The skies over our union suffered from a lack of stars, and I did not know how to bring them back, how to find the light.

And suddenly I was using a new colour to paint my painting, a colour I had never used before: the colour of lies.

Lies are blue. Blue, like the eyes of Sergei Krasin. This lie is Russian and it lives at 14, rue Jacob.

During Kamran's absences, I would see his friends or his business colleagues. I did not see anyone whom I had not met through him. This does not mean I was a submissive wife, a prisoner; on the contrary, it was always me organising the dinners, the parties, the whole 'social' aspect of our life as a couple. I did not feel I needed to have other friends outside this particular sphere. My father and mother were enough for me. And then there were books, films, art exhibitions. I couldn't ask for anything better. Every day I would go to the big bookshop on the boulevard Raspail, where I'd been in charge of the Foreign Literature section for the past seven years. I liked the job very much, it allowed me to meet interesting people while letting me pursue my passion for reading. I was 'in books' like a fish is in water: free and untroubled. I didn't talk to my colleagues much, and at lunch I usually went out alone to the corner bistro for a sandwich. No one knew that my husband was an editor. When I unpacked boxes of his books I was delighted, and when one of his books sold well or got on to the bestseller lists, I was delighted, but discreetly, in silence. No one could know. For some reason, I wanted this anonymity. I needed there to be a separation between my professional activities and Kamran's, even if we discussed literature each evening, commenting on the latest arrivals. He would ask my opinion of foreign titles he was considering for his publishing house, and I was pleased he thought me a good enough reader to be able to comment. I was thrilled to notice he usually followed my advice.

My colleagues respected my reserve. They labelled me the 'slightly uptight girl', but this severe, not very flattering nickname actually pleased me more than it irritated me. Sometimes I wanted to say: 'I'm really not uptight at all, just secretive,' but I didn't, fearing I would come off as arrogant. I was sociable enough, and they eventually got used to my being different. In any case, my seniority, and the fact that I was the only salesperson to speak many languages fluently, made things a lot easier. During school breaks and the holidays, temps would come in. 'Badly paid and boring,' they would say, giving back their overalls after a few days.

I love books. As long as they are there, arranged in alphabetical order on the shelves of the bookshop, laid out on the coffee table in our living room, piled on the floor in our bedroom – as long as I had a book in my hands, I felt safe. Books speak to me, and I answer them, in fact my relationship to them was nearly physical. I owed them my tears, my good cheer, my tenderness, my sensuality. I walked amongst and inside words whenever I wanted, with the certainty that at the end of the page, the chapter, the ballad, the quatrain, pleasure would carry me far, very far away. I took notes and stored up knowledge with the devotion of a schoolgirl. I'd pull out one sentence, an expression, which I would write down in one of those little notebooks, one of those 'one year of white pages' notebooks or those famous moleskin notebooks Ernest Hemingway used to carry – which of course we sell at the bookshop. Yes, I love books and everything that goes with them. 'You should write, really write,' Kamran would say when he saw me scribbling away in my notebooks. Write? No, I'd much rather read the words of others, it's less dangerous.

I dislike being alone on Sundays. When Kamran is out of town – which is rare since he knows how melancholic I get on Sundays – I usually cross the street to visit my parents, who also happen to live on the boulevard Saint-Germain. My mother cooks Iranian food, my father talks about politics or about Persian poetry; we light candles, watch videos, we laugh, play cards, and I lose, almost always.

But that Sunday evening my parents were gone, they had decided to go to Morocco for a few days. They are usually reluctant to leave me alone when Kamran is out of town, but I had encouraged them to go. I was just about to get into bed with a novel when the telephone rang; it was probably Kamran wanting to tell me about his day, making sure I was not too bored. I picked up the phone, speaking cheerfully, as do all Iranian women who refuse to whine about their lives. *'Never explain, never complain.'* But the voice I heard was that of an old girlfriend, Valarie, whose husband, an Englishman, had studied business law at the same university as Kamran. They were still close friends. I had become good friends with Valarie and we often dined as a threesome. Valarie and Mark were the perfect couple, both lawyers, with two children and a beautiful house in the suburbs west of Paris.

'Roxane, it's Valarie! We're at the Brasserie Lipp. Kamran mentioned you were going to be alone, come and join us for dinner!'

'I don't know, it's raining and I don't much feel like going out . . . '

'No, you must come, it's an order!'

So I did. I grabbed my bag and my raincoat and checked my hair in the hall mirror, slamming the door on the way out.

Outside it was cool, rather nice, a real spring evening. I had slept for most of the afternoon. The asphalt shimmered from a recent shower, a few raindrops caught the back of my neck. I pulled out my silk scarf and tied it around my hair, which was wild and wavy with the humidity. I laughed out loud, thinking what my mother, a flirt like all Iranian women, used to say to me when I was a teenager: 'Roxane, when your hair looks good, so will the rest of you.' The boulevard Saint-Germain, so animated in the daytime with its boutiques and cafés, looked like a long empty tunnel. Ten minutes later I arrived at the brasserie where Valarie and Mark were waiting for me. A lot of people were queuing outside, but my friends had reserved a corner table, from which they were waving at me. I was excited to see them, they had just come back from a week's vacation in the mountains, looking tanned and bright-eyed. Mark gallantly ushered me in to sit next to Valarie on the banquette. Behind us was a giant mirror in which I saw the reflection of more than half the people in the brasserie. And then I saw him. I saw the colour of danger, the colour of lies. *Blue.* I felt this blue-grey colour jolt into my heart, this blue which was like a Chinese ink-painting from the Xing dynasty, the mountain landscapes painted across a thirteen-metre horizontal roll in all the evolving nuances of grey: a stream dries up and a sacred terrace emerges, a vision of the skies appears with mountains, hills, celestial pathways.

I saw him, and the sight took my breath away. I barely heard the question I was being asked: 'And for madame?'

And then the teasing voice of Valarie: 'Madame is with her books . . . '

I looked down at the menu I was holding, trying to decipher it, the long list of appetisers, entrées and desserts, the lines jumbling together like a vast and stormy sea. Something violent had just happened to me, across from me, sitting at another table for three. I say 'violent' because I did not expect to be so struck, again, by a mere look. It had happened once and once only, when my eyes had met Kamran's. Since then I had met the gaze of many other men, but my heart and body did not respond to anyone except Kamran. With a husband who was frequently away on business, it would have been easy to become one of those Parisian mistresses, going out for nooners instead of for lunch. I never looked back at those men, wanting to stay permanently connected to Kamran, the man of my life. The idea of betraying or deceiving him was repugnant. I knew he was faithful to our commitment, which went far beyond the sacred bonds of marriage. Exile gives a different dimension to love, rendering it guilty, placing it on a pedestal, idealising it beyond all reason. I didn't want to belong to any other man but Kamran. Even after fourteen years of married life, even after our disappointment at not being able to build the family we both dreamed about. Suddenly, I heard myself say: 'Oh, I would like a *sole meurnière* and a green salad . . . '

I didn't even know if these items were on the menu. I remembered another dinner I had eaten at this brasserie, so I ordered the exact same thing.

'Don't you want to try something else?' asked Valarie, who had been at that other dinner as well.

'No, I assure her, I'm really not that hungry . . . '

Realising that my friends were starting to look at me a little oddly, I began speaking very quickly, louder than I usually did. My voice and laugh sounded artificial – but little by little the atmosphere went back to normal and they began telling me about their holiday, their children; I heard perhaps one word out of three. Our conversation almost disappeared, since my responses were delayed. I hated myself for deceiving my friends, and perhaps I would have returned to the world of reason if those blue eyes had turned away from mine, if the man sitting across from me had been concentrating on what was happening at his own table. Instead he was multi-tasking with disconcerting ease, eating – they were already having their desserts, while we had just ordered – smiling at me, smiling at his friends, smiling at me again, pretending to look interested in the photographs his friends were showing him, smiling at me again, eating a little, talking a lot, lighting a cigarette, putting it out when the maître d' asked him to. As he stubbed out his cigarette he sent me a secret smile, as if to say: 'This is a non-smoking area, but I bet you really want a cigarette too.' I smiled back at him and Valarie thought I was agreeing with whatever she had just said. I had no idea what it was, but apparently my agreement was the right answer. Fascinated, I could not take my eyes off his moving hands as he was talking to his friends: in this rhythmic choreography I saw both purity and delicacy, rage and passion.

'They say you get hungry as you eat,' said Mark, 'and it's true. You inhaled that salad as though you hadn't eaten for a week!'

I laughed, muttering excuses.

'When Kamran is out of town I only eat when I happen to think of it . . . '

What I really wanted was to hurry things along, since I could see that the trio at the other table was getting ready to order the traditional 'three coffees and the check, please'. Those blue eyes were going to abandon me. 'No, no, wait! Wait for me!' I said with my eyes. Then, suddenly surprised by own audacity, I turned abruptly back to my friends. They had now moved on to discussing a film they had seen, which happily I had seen also.

'Roxane! Roxane, are you all right? You look so strange all of a sudden . . . '

I jumped, probably looking quite strange. Valarie continued: 'And weren't you supposed to join Kamran in Madrid?'

I realised I had better pull myself together. My skin felt hot, I was shaking. The palms of my hands were damp. I picked up a piece of bread and tore it into little pieces, then took a sip of white wine. It was delicious, slightly sweet, reminding me of Iran. I knew that Mark had ordered it especially for me, to please me. The wine calmed me a little, but also made me feel the heat. I thought about Kamran, the man I had been promised to at the age of twelve. I could never, I would never hurt him. Valarie and Mark could ask me questions all night and they would learn nothing from me. I was master of my own soul, it was mine. Leaving my country had taught me this.

'Yes, I was supposed to go to Madrid, but I don't know if it's possible. We're short staffed at the bookshop and I am just so tired.'

Tired, yes. But above all, unsettled. Valarie didn't see it. She said, sadly: 'It's too bad, maybe the two of you would have had some time to yourselves. But – sorry – I'm sticking my nose where it doesn't belong. It's just that you so rarely show what you are feeling. I admire you, you never complain, you never show anyone how you are suffering.'

'Stop! I'm certainly not the perfect woman you are describing . . . '

Especially since I am lying, shaking as I face the intensity of this man I know nothing about . . .

They are getting ready to leave. The bill is paid, the coffee cups are empty. The cloakroom attendant has brought them their raincoats. There was only one solution to the problem. It was a miserable, shameful choice, but there was nothing else to be done.

'Valarie, I'm going to go. I have an early start tomorrow, so . . . '

'Sure, I understand. Mark and I weren't planning to have dessert, so we'll drive you home.'

I cut her off: 'No, don't worry about it, I'd actually rather walk. A little fresh air would do me good, it's so hot in here . . . '

They stared at me, surprised. Valarie especially – women have a sixth sense when it comes to this sort of thing! I grab my raincoat off the banquette and put it on while looking casually towards the revolving door. The three of them are laughing as they go out. I pull out my purse to pay for my share of the dinner, but Mark shakes his head: 'Don't even think about it! Take care of yourself, Roxane. We'll see you when Kamran is back.'

'Good-night and thank you so much!'

I hug them and promise to call if I don't feel well later on tonight. My heart is already outside, where his heart is. I am ashamed. All that I am not, all that I have always refused to be, I am now becoming. It is vulgar, cowardly, impure. I am ready to exchange the blueness of my Iranian sky, for another blue, clearer and more transparent, yet somehow deeper. I could drown myself in that blue. I stammer a pathetic 'good-night', barely managing not to trip on the overhanging tablecloth, stumbling a little, hoping Valarie and Mark will attribute my bizarre behaviour to the fatigue I mentioned earlier.

Has he understood what I am about to do? A few metres from the restaurant, he is delaying, still standing with his friends. I know that he's seen me, yet he does not walk away from his friends – I suppose that saying goodbye always takes more time than you expect. Perhaps he doesn't dare make the first move towards me, but his reserve is like a slap in the face for me. If he doesn't dare, how will I be able to? I have already gone so far beyond reason. Still, I take several steps in his direction, feeling as if I am tainting my honour in some way. Finally, the trio separates. He seems to hesitate. He crushes his cigarette butt on the pavement and crosses the boulevard Saint-Germain against the light. I want to shout, 'Watch out!' even though the street is empty. I wait for the light to change before I follow him. He walks slowly, his shoulders hunched inside the collar of his raincoat, occasionally glancing to the left and then to the right, perhaps looking for an open *tabac,* or maybe for a way to get rid of this annoying woman following him, her pride forgotten. He must be thinking this woman is so desperate, she will go out to meet a stranger. No, maybe he is wondering how to approach me. What is he waiting for? It is strange, but without knowing it he is walking in the direction of my house. Soon we arrive in front of the Eglise Saint-Germain. My high heels are tapping sharply on the cobblestones.

I am making a noise, but it doesn't matter, he knows I am there. I am still following him and I feel he knows it. We are in my neighbourhood. If he takes the rue Bonaparte, he'll pass in front of a *bar tabac* which stays open very late. I lay out this itinerary for him in my head and he seems to hear it. How can we counter these signs of destiny? And why fight them? As I'd hoped, he takes the rue Bonaparte, walking quickly as if he'd seen the sign for the *tabac*. I stop at the corner, waiting for him, my heart pounding. When he comes out he will have to speak to me, or maybe he'll give me the brush-off, tell me to go away. 'No, you can't do this,' a voice whispers to me. I step back into the shadows, slipping into a doorway. I am torn, in two minds, finding it impossible simply to say: '*If Allah Wills It!*' I pull myself together. The rain clears my head, and I lift my face to receive it like a sort of celestial punishment.

It happened so quickly, I couldn't have stopped it. I am standing there, hidden, ashamed, raindrops and tears running down my face, uneasy inside my contradictory desires as one might feel uncomfortable inside a particularly tight garment. I see him coming out on to the quai carrying several packs of cigarettes. He pulls a lighter out of his pocket and continues walking while trying to light one in spite of the rain. I am frozen and incapable of making any decisions, so I watch him moving farther and farther away from the pavement, absorbed in his need for a smoke. Suddenly a car comes speeding out of the night, then it disappears. The young man cries out before he falls, his forehead slamming into the asphalt. I run towards him.

I kneel, taking his face between my hands. With my fingers I feel his cold neck, see the line of blood running along his temple.

I was born daughter and mother at the same time, child and woman. I do my duty, that is all.

Later that night, when I got home, the painting of my life had reverted to the blank canvas it used to be. This was a new beginning. My bloodstained clothes and silk scarf were proof of that. I wanted to lie on my bed in these soiled clothes. To fall asleep like that, without listening to the messages on the machine, without putting the light on, without washing, without eating. Tomorrow I would go to the hospital.

It was dark in the living room. I had forgotten that I'd closed the curtains before going out with Valarie and Mark. The dimness, in which objects and furniture seemed to float between dream and reality, felt like a continuation of what had just happened. Too much light would have brought me abruptly back to reality. I wanted to stay inside what Thomas Mann calls the impossible space of unspeakable desire. I had just found all three of them together – the impossible, the space, and the desire – which was both intoxicating and terrifying.

I went into the kitchen and poured myself a glass of red wine, then carried it into my room. I took a sip, then another, very quickly. I was thirsty. In my hurry I had spilled a little wine, and a couple of drops fell on to the cover of a book I had started reading the day before. I put the wine glass down on the night table, covered with newspapers and magazines, lighting a half-burned candle. The flame was small, then suddenly leaped up through its golden screen, revealing the contours of your sweet face to me once more. I sank back into the past as I might take my seat at the cinema. With the colour red dominating, always. I lay down on my bed, crossing my hands on my belly, and began to touch your forehead, your mouth, your hands. Your fingers grazed my lips, cooled by the breeze. I felt the heat of your breath. I spoke to you, and said: 'Everything you forget is mine,' and it was true, because when we were both in that taxi, I took possession of your shadows. I searched what you didn't say as one would dig in the earth to bury a great treasure. Our secrets will be safe, trust me.

Tomorrow is today, and I will run after your light and attempt to catch it. It will be a child's game, or perhaps an adult game. The uncertainty terrifies and warms me at the same time. Today, I may hear the sound of your voice.

When the telephone rang, I thought it was you, and I didn't know if I should say hello, goodbye, or farewell.

'Roxane?' A voice repeats, 'Roxane?'

Answering this voice I do not recognise, I say: 'I think the car was white, yes, white.'

'What car? Roxane? It's me, Kamran. Are you all right?'

I hold the receiver, which I grabbed automatically, against my ear. Apparently I am often distracted and absent, which is why people have to say my name two, even three times to get my attention. It doesn't bother me. Each time it is as if I were coming up to the surface after having flirted with the deep for a long time; I need a couple of seconds to get myself sorted out. It has been like this since I was a child.

'Roxane! Ro–xa–ne!' My parents used to yell my name out in the warm hallways and the aromatic nooks of our house in Tehran; I would stay hidden in the shadows of the fig, linden and walnut trees, my heart pounding, my soul vibrating with the thousand worrisome dreams I used to tell my adored trees – I have always loved trees and sought their protection, for me their roots are the tangible antithesis of exile, whether it be in Iran or in Paris on the place Saint-Germain. Trees do not move. They are exposed to so many dangers, yet they barely tremble when the great storms come. In Iran, some of them, the old ones, planted near the mausoleums of the saints and the poets, are considered sacred; people tie strips of fabric to their branches, hoping their wishes will be granted. The Koran compares the word of God to a tree whose celestial branches connect to deep roots, and which gives fruit in all seasons . . . Anyway, after having discussed things with my precious allies the trees, I would appear with a twinkling laugh, twirling around to show my tenth new dress of the week, before announcing: 'I'm here!' with a studied candour. I was happy: I was being scolded, so I existed. I talked to the sun, to the sea, to the flora and fauna. I told them, 'I love you,' as if knowing I would have to leave them behind one day. For a long time, perhaps for ever. I was rehearsing my exile, performing my farewell scene ahead of time, imagining my voice reverberating around the forests, south of the Caspian Sea, up to the Zagros mountains, before fading away into the salty deserts. When I bleed, it is not blood that flows, it is really my childhood, that childhood.

I ask in a sleepy voice: 'What time is it?'

'Eight o'clock! Normally you're in the shower at this time. Did I wake you?'

'Yes, I mean – no.'

'What's going on, you sound bizarre . . . '

The word 'bizarre' shocked me out of my torpor. I must not seem too bizarre. I must return to being a young woman who is happy when her husband calls her. I am, in fact, quite happy to hear his voice, but am having difficulty separating 'last night' from 'this morning'. I would love to be spontaneous, to be able to say to him, 'Guess what, yesterday I saved the life of a man I didn't know,' but at the same time I know that the lie is going to win out over the truth.

'I tried to reach you last night . . . what did you do?'

'Valarie and Mark invited me to dinner with them at the Brasserie Lipp. I was all ready for bed, and then . . . '

'You were right to go, I don't like you moping around

when I'm not there, especially when your parents aren't there either. Have you arranged it with the bookshop that you can come down to Madrid? We could take some time just for us, go to the galleries, the exhibitions, you could clear your head a little.'

Leave Paris now? Give up the hope of diving once more into the blue of his eyes? Turning my head, I catch my reflection in an old mirror that is hung above a chest of rare wood, a souvenir of my maternal grandmother. Who is this woman in the mirror who looks so dazed, her hair all messed up, her lips tight? My eyes move to my wrinkled raincoat, the silk scarf I am still wearing around my neck. Is it me, or a vagabond lady, or perhaps a party girl who has just stumbled home after a raucous night? I swallow painfully and get hold of myself, attempting to get back into the conversation.

'How was your dinner with that writer you so wanted to meet?'

The sound of my own voice annoys me. I can hear myself, and my cheeks flush. I am acting, badly, and yet somehow Kamran does not notice. I realise there is indeed a manual for deceit, and I have pressed all the right buttons.

'I managed to convince him he'd be better off with me. His transfer is going to cost me a lot of money, and I don't much like having authors break their contracts, but on the whole I am satisfied.'

And I reply quickly, trying to hide my confusion. I am

cursing myself for the pathetic set of lies I am laying down in blue ink. They are for you, or perhaps for us.

'That's great, I'm so happy for you.'

'You know, Roxane, it doesn't matter if you don't come to Madrid, we'll have other opportunities.'

'You're not too disappointed?'

'No, don't worry about it. But, what was that thing about a white car?'

'Oh, nothing, just a bad dream.'

'Good, fine. I'm off then, I'm already late. So are you, I think.'

'You're right, I'd better call the bookshop.'

'OK. I'll call you tomorrow. Since you're not coming down I should be home on Friday, during the day . . . '

I hang up the phone with a sigh of relief. Now, even before I take my shower, I must start the second part of my itinerary of lies. At least this time it is easier. I take the telephone into the kitchen, and before I call the bookshop I drink a big glass of water. I get the director on the line. He's a nice, unsuspecting man who likes me and appreciates my work. I tell him I am coming down with a kind of gastroenteritis, and of course he tells me to stay at home and stay warm. He tells me he can handle things without me the next day too, if I don't feel better. I thank him for his understanding and hang up, feeling a little ashamed. At the same time I have no reason to feel guilty. I have been a model employee, punctual, cheerful, willing to do overtime whenever it is necessary. I like what I do and I am not someone who would ask for time off if I had a cold. I often even work six-day weeks.

I begin by getting rid of my clothes. I thought I would do what they do in the movies: taking them to be cleaned at an anonymous dry-cleaners. I should be able to pick them up before Kamran's return, on Friday. I turn the radio on to wake myself up, to bring me back to reality: not music, the news. I want the words of other people to slam into my words, the ones ricocheting around my head. 'A white car? Yes, it was a white car . . . ' So what? There are thousands of white cars circulating in the streets of Paris. I go into the bathroom, turn on the shower, exposing my face, my hair and my body to the purifying water. For a long time I stay like that, my head flung back, my eyes half-closed, trying to distance myself from everything except the water, which I want to be boiling hot or freezing cold, splashing my face before streaming down my back. Then I come out of the shower, wrapping myself in a bathrobe. I dry my hair and finally dare to look in the mirror again. I must have slept two or three hours, no more, and that's exactly what it looks like. I have large black circles of mascara around my eyes. 'Are you still governed by reason?' I thought, looking at my pitiful reflection. Since I was now anticipating Kamran's return, I was no longer thinking about his telephone call. Instead I was thinking about the instant his eyes and mine would meet, how I would put my head down on his shoulder and ask if he had had a good trip.

And he would say, kindly: 'Darling, is everything OK with you?' I counted all the little betrayals which would now be punctuating my sentences. I would show him my gentleness, and he would accept it, misunderstanding it, telling himself he'd married a wonderful young woman – something of a dreamer, baffling, unpredictable, even secretive sometimes, with an imagination that was perhaps a bit more developed than others – but so generous and loving, so protective. He would smile and his honeyed eyes would speak to me about our childish games, our vows, our plans, the trips we would take, wherever and whenever I wanted. I was so small and he was a giant. Kamran's wide, strong, powerful hands – so different from Sergei's, who had adolescent hands – they would caress my hair. 'Like silk,' Kamran would say, unrolling each curl with his fingers, before adding in an admiring tone, 'What is your secret?' About my secrets, though, I would remain silent, pressing myself against him. And then . . .

Two long hours later, I had finally pulled myself together. Of course, in this circumstance the expression 'to pull myself together' was laughable, because I was still in a highly agitated state. My hair was done, my make-up was done, I was dressed and ready to go. Of course, I knew I would be going towards the hospital – in fact there was a bus, the No. 63, which stopped near my building and would get me there in less than fifteen minutes. During the trip I would have plenty of time to consider how to present myself. I was technically the only witness to the accident. The taxi driver had offered his help when Sergei was already lying on the ground. Had the staff at the café where he bought those cigarettes – had they seen something? Unlikely, since the *bar tabac* was a rather poor observation point. In any case, it was too late to give a statement at the police station. Its lateness would immediately render it suspect, and it would put me in a delicate position. I did not want to reveal my identity. At the same time, I asked myself if Sergei had any family in Paris. If he did, they would have already tried to find them, beginning in the early morning. By going to the hospital I was risking coming face to face with one of his friends or relatives. I did not want Sergei to know I was the one who had saved him. Had I really saved him? Had he woken up? And if he had, had they transferred him to a different ward? Perhaps even to another hospital? Perhaps I should go directly to his home at 14 rue Jacob? I could talk to the shopkeepers, to his neighbours? But no, I would not become involved in his private life. I did not have the right. Who was I to him? Was I a part of his unconscious now, since watching him sleep? I would have liked for him to make a small place for me in his memory, so he could say when he woke up, 'I think I was not alone; there was someone else with me.' Living in his memory for eternity would be enough for me.

Tired of repeating the same questions, I decided to let myself be guided by instinct, although taking care to avoid the boulevard Raspail and its area. I was so distracted, so blown away by the intensity of the last twenty-four hours that I could see myself going to get a coffee in one of the bars near the bookshop! It was abnormally warm for the season, 20°C outside they said on the radio. I did not only need my sunglasses to protect me from the brightness, though. I liked the idea that you would have priority over my eyes, with their weary eyelids. If you were going to wake up and see me, I wanted for you to see something no one else had seen that day before you, not the *gardienne* in my building, not the bus driver or his passengers, or the passers-by; no one, no one except you would reach through my eyes into the depths of my soul.

Often it takes only a tiny detail to bring two beings together. The smallest things change our lives, and turn us away from a path we had planned out. A minute speck, a spark, can grow into a flame. Passion is more intense than reality. It goes beyond it. Maybe we don't realise that such passion burns in each of us, and that it may propel us into an unknown future, free of all constraints. Passion is a magnet, we follow it instinctively. When established, it has power over our behaviour. This is how I understood the events that changed my life.

I picked up the plastic bag containing my raincoat, blouse and silk scarf, all of which I was going to take to the cleaners. I slammed the door of my flat in the way you slam the door on a hotel room where you've spent only a few hours, feeling a sudden emptiness, a familiar feeling from the more painful moments of my exile. Running down the stairs, I imagined something to give you besides my gaze, words that would be a sort of a bridge from one exile to another, something I would like to recite to you on the day you share with me the poems of Pablo Neruda. On that day, if God gave it to me, I would speak to you of Omar Khayyam, one of the great Persian poets. I whispered one of his quatrains, one of the many I know by heart:

> We are all toys in the hands of Heaven
> Which moves us as He wishes: He is our master.
> In the game of chess, we are eternal pawns,
> Falling one after the other deep inside nothingness.

Everyone hates the smell of the hospital. Everyone except me, at the exact moment I step inside. And as long as you are inside these walls, you will belong to me. Hospitals are all alike. From the outside they look like fortresses. In theory, when you ask to enter different buildings you are asked for an ID and have to pass through various hurdles before being allowed in. Yet in practice you can walk around day and night without arousing any suspicions, if you know how to do it. It's easy as long as you don't use the lifts reserved for the patients and the staff, and as long as you know where you are going. You walk quietly, staying close to the walls, speaking as little as possible. You don't ask questions, you figure stuff out for yourself. I arrive in the lobby and immediately see that I won't have to fight too hard to get to you. I say your name to the two ladies behind the information desk, my stomach in knots, my throat tight. One of them glances at me, then looks at her in-patient list, sighing: 'Krasin with a C or with a K?'

'With a K,' I whisper back.

'Sergei Krasin, Building C, third floor, room 334,' she says without even looking at me.

I thank her and go off towards Building C. So you're not in Intensive Care any more. Does this mean you have regained consciousness? With my heart pounding, I move quickly through the large courtyard until I am standing in front of Building C. I am drenched in sweat. I suddenly feel like turning around. I know the hardest part is coming, the moment when a nurse or an orderly will approach me with the customary, 'Are you family?' And I would not be able to lie. My watch reads exactly noon. I am relying on the staff being out on their lunch break in order to sneak up to Room 334. Usually they bring the patients their lunch trays around 11 a.m., so I need to make the most of the time I have. I slide into the lift, happy to be in there by myself. Holding my breath, I press the button for the third floor. My destiny depends on this door opening. I can feel a vein throbbing in my temple, a drop of perspiration rolls down the back of my neck, my hands are like ice. I have to warm them, otherwise I will not be able to touch your face. I am obsessed by the idea that you might be cold, feel cold. Inside and outside. A slight jolt tells me I have arrived, the old metal door slides open so slowly I can't stand it. On this floor, everything is old, broken, damaged, filthy. Everything reeks of disinfectant, but that bothers me less than the general dilapidation. It's as if there has been an earthquake on each floor, everything seems stuck, heavy, oppressive. As I step out, I nearly collide with a nurse and her trolley, but she pays me no attention whatsoever. I feel like I have entered a large, grey street, flanked with a lot of numbered pathways. At the end of the 'street', I see a sort of dayroom for patients who are ambulatory. I immediately check out the nurses' station, whose door is wide open. I can hear laughter, covered by the sound of a television turned up loud. 'Turn that down!' a woman yells from somewhere on the ward. I stay close to the pale-green wall as I approach Room 334. The glass door is closed. I listen for a second. Nothing. No noise. Rising on to my toes, I peep in through the frosted-glass window. I see two beds. I can't stand it. I open the door, thinking that none of this seems real. I am sneaking into a hospital room to steal a moment of sleep from an unknown man. Nobody would believe it, except maybe Kamran, who knows me better than anyone, who knows I am capable of intoxicating myself with the irrational. Only he knows this. Sometimes I see in his eyes that this excessive side of me scares him. He doesn't say anything. His refusal to speak about the depths of the passion that I have never stopped seeking involves neither cowardice nor complaisance. Kamran thinks I want to stay inside the painting I began at the age of twelve. He was right. And also wrong. 'Please, forgive me if you can,' I begged as I pushed the door open.

There you are. Unconscious. Lying on your back, your arms crossed over your chest. In the other bed there is another man with brown hair, around thirty, also asleep. If a member of your family comes in, I can always pretend to be visiting the other patient.

I take off my sunglasses and approach you, my arms dangling, suddenly feeling rather lost. I don't dare breathe, I am worried you will wake up in the next minute. You look like you're dreaming, like you just lay down for a nap. One more step and I am close, so close to you. The hem of my jacket grazes the white sheet which covers you up to the chin, where I can see the edge of your green hospital gown. Suddenly I am overcome by emotion. I bring my hand towards your face, but – I don't dare. My fingers tremble over your skin, as thin as onion-skin paper, hovering over landscapes, rivers, towns, transparencies, turbulences. My hand, dazzled, stops in mid-flight. A non-stop flight without borders and without anger since our two countries are meeting each other in complete serenity and freedom. Skin against skin, blood against blood, or almost. My olive Iranian skin against the pale whiteness of your Russian skin. I've never been particularly good at geography, but I know that we share, you and I, a bit of the Caspian Sea . . .

I burn, wanting to touch you. I must not. I already know your face with its fine bone structure, and I can visualise your slim body through the sheet. Our eyes met on that rainy Sunday, but I know nothing about your voice. Is it deep or high-pitched, warm or cold, melodious or monotonous? How does it sound when you are angry or you burst into laughter? Does it show sympathy, emotion, tenderness? Who is it that you answer, who do you whisper and sigh with, the way you are sighing now? You are probably too young to have children, but I can easily see you with a wife, a mistress, a close female friend. The other night at the restaurant, I felt a solitude in your gaze, I know that laughing with friends means nothing. Appearing to be happy is not difficult, even when you've been totally destroyed on the inside.

I am waiting for a voice, *your* voice. In a little while when I am back home I will make it up, imagine it, render it accessible by the pure force of my will. You are going to live, Sergei, it doesn't matter if it is not for me. Because one spring Sunday night I said farewell to you before I said hello. You will live, because you are an exile and an exile is born to fight, to fight against despair and to cultivate hope. This survival is in your genes.

Suddenly, as I stand there, frozen and quiet, my hands suspended over the untouched territory of your handsome face, I hear a disturbance in the hall. Immediately I back away from the bed and move towards the door, my heart pounding. Someone is going to find me, I think, terrified. Then the noise, apparently nothing more than the collision of two nurses' trolleys, stops. A short exchange between the two nurses tells me I have nothing to fear, and once again the room fills with silence. I glance quickly at the other patient, who is moaning at regular intervals. Unlike you, he seems to be suffering, battling his darkest demons.

From time to time his arms and his legs quiver, his mouth twists – I am sure he is going to open his eyes and glare at me. I send you a kiss with my fingers. 'Before I met you, my dreams were more beautiful than my reality,' I murmur, as a wave of heat rushes through my body. How can I say such unjust words? But it is true. I am fully aware of it in this hospital room. For the first time in my whole life I am living an extraordinary situation, in the literal sense of the word. My daily life before this was so banal. Comfortable, from a material point of view, but banal, insubstantial. 'How many children do you want?' Kamran asked me at the very beginning of our marriage. 'As many as there are stars in the sky!' I answered grandly. Kamran laughed, he had always wanted a big family – and the memory of that cheerful laugh is killing me, little by little. We will never have any stars, not one. Kamran does not want to adopt, and I understand his reasons, which I share. We do not have the strength to live another exile through a child not our own.

Ashamed of my descent into self-pity in this place where so many lives are ending in silence, I swallow my sobs. I open the door a crack and check out the corridor. No one. I put my sunglasses back on and walk quickly towards the lift, my head down.

I walked for a long time in the overheated streets and as usual I got lost, on purpose. The sky was no longer the colour of your eyes. And grey is a poor guide.

It is because of Heaven that I am so fierce.
It is Heaven which tore my happiness into shreds.
The air blowing on me is like the fire
>   from a giant torch
And water now tastes like dirt in my mouth.

Sergei, I speak to you and I will speak to you until my dying day, until I have gone through the poetry collections of the entire world. Because you are a poet, I am sure. Did you know that in Iran, the poets give the title of 'garden' to their body of work?

Since I left the hospital, a song has filled my head. This song – I remember hearing it in the taxi that memorable Sunday night. I focus on the film it is from, trying to remember where I saw it for the first time. Finally, as I approached the Pont-Neuf, I remembered. A colleague at the bookshop, a film buff and an admirer of Romy Schneider, had lent me a VHS copy of the film, a few months ago, saying: 'You'll see, this story is for you.' A story for me – yes, now I remember. I watched that film one night when I couldn't sleep. Kamran was on a trip to New York, and he had forgotten the time difference. He woke me up and I couldn't get back to sleep. I remember being totally absorbed by the story, something about the complexity of our destinies, and I was especially impressed with the powerful acting of Michel Piccoli and Romy Schneider. The next day, still mesmerised – the night renders our emotions so much more dramatic – I wanted to return the video cassette to my colleague, but she refused, saying it was a gift. I was touched by her gesture. I saw the film a second time, and cried my eyes out. But I had no idea where I'd put the video. I knew I had not lent it to anyone, and I knew that Kamran had not watched it – he was not interested in this kind of psychological drama. No, I didn't have any idea where I'd put it. Walking quickly across the Pont-Neuf, I realised I was approaching the rue Jacob. My head was spinning. I was no longer lost, I was already haunted by the idea of losing Sergei, and I wanted to get closer to him, by whatever means possible. I was looking for him. Had I already begun missing him? Confused, I stopped and leaned on the stone balustrade of the bridge, staring down at the *bateaux-mouches,* those little floating houses visited each day by hundreds of strangers, gliding gracefully by on the Seine, with its shining, metallic reflections.

Roland Barthes wrote in *A Lover's Discourse: Fragments*:

And long after the love relationship has cooled, I continue the habit of imagining the person I loved. Sometimes I still worry about a late telephone call, and no matter who is on the line, I seem to recognise the voice that I once loved: I am an amputee who continues to feel pain in the missing leg.

This sentence had touched me, I had written it in my notebook, I saw myself in it, the words defined me. When

Sergei wakes up, he will remember nothing. He will have forgotten me. Full stop.

'Roxane, which do you prefer, books or life?' Valarie asked me one day, at an art opening we had attended, together with Mark, Kamran, and two other couples. 'Life, of course!' I snapped. Everyone laughed and Valarie looked at me strangely. She had that same expression, intrigued and incredulous, at the restaurant that Sunday when I left the table so precipitately. She said: 'Still waters run deep, you know . . . '

Now I was standing at one end of the rue Jacob. Near his building. No to go up to Number 14 would be ridiculous, I thought, as I strode along the pavement on the even-numbered side of the street. I stopped a little before Number 10. I was frozen, at once scared and careful. I looked left, then right, then directly at Sergei's building, a few steps from where I stood. Its façade was being renovated, showing the age of the building. Several workmen were moving around the scaffolding. I walked directly towards them without hesitating, perhaps one of them would be able to give me some information about my handsome stranger.

'Good-morning, sir, I . . . I'm looking for a young man,' I stammered. 'He lives here in this building. He's around twenty-five years old, blond, not too tall, quite thin, with blue eyes. Do you think you might have seen him?'

'No, no, I haven't seen anything,' he said in an unfriendly voice. 'Sorry, lady, I have work to do.'

'Yes, of course, excuse me.'

I tried my luck with the older man who seemed to be in charge of the renovation.

'A young man with blue eyes? No, no, I don't think so. In any case, we don't look at who is going in and out, you know.'

I realised I would learn nothing from these men. Feeling a little silly, I turned around. I didn't dare enter the building, much less talk to the *gardienne*. I looked for a café or a *bar tabac*. These places, like taxis, are information gold mines. Often the owners won't tell you anything, but sometimes they do. I forced a smile and pushed open the door to the one that was closest to Number 14, hoping that Sergei had been in there to order a coffee or a pack of cigarettes. I stepped up to the counter and ordered some tea. I was about to light a cigarette, when the waiter said: 'Sorry, madame, you can't smoke here.'

'Oh! Sorry, it's instinctive,' I said, embarrassed.

He seemed rather bored, listlessly wiping dry the glasses he was taking out of the dishwasher. I seized the occasion, exchanging a few banalities, then asking him the same question: 'Have you by any chance . . . ? A young man with blond hair and blue eyes, living at No. 14?' His, 'Yes, sure,' blew me away, as I had expected a negative answer. I took a sip of tea to recover my composure, but the waiter continued, in an entirely unexpected way, that yes, he did in fact know Sergei, 'a nice young man, rather shy, with a slight accent'. The waiter had served him several times, although Sergei was not a regular. He came in from time to time for a coffee and to buy his cigarettes. Apparently he was always carrying notebooks and books, which he sometimes dropped. In general he came in alone, except for a couple of times when he was with a blonde girl, a little older than him. They seemed close, but the barman could not ascertain the exact nature of their relationship. A woman? I was shaken. So Sergei did have someone in his life. What could be more normal? I had expected it, but . . . The barman was on a roll, continuing to give me more details. It all fitted perfectly. I put some change on the counter to pay for my tea. He looked at me: 'In fact, now that you mention it, I haven't seen him for about two weeks. I usually see him every day, sometimes he waves at me. Is he . . . ?'

I didn't let him finish the sentence. I didn't want to give him the time to speculate about me or my questions.

As I walked away I thought about continuing my investigation. I could talk to all the shopkeepers in the area, beginning with the little stationery shop at the corner of the rue Bonaparte. I could go to the post office, the bakery, to the neighbourhood Monoprix, to the Sorbonne. I could cover all the streets, retrace the route we had taken, checking each place he might have left a trace. I thought about it, but then gave up, suddenly heartsick. It was because of the blonde girl mentioned by the barman. I could not just pretend that she didn't exist. And I could not go looking for him, not now.

Discouraged and slightly disoriented, I slowed down a little. As I walked back up the rue Bonaparte towards the place Saint-Germain, by now deeply despondent, I thought about the next day, about having to face my colleagues at the bookshop, avoiding their questions as usual. Should I continue to simulate having gastro-enteritis to get another day off? No, I really couldn't. I didn't like lying. And my apparent skill as an amateur liar devastated me. Kamran did not deserve this. No one deserves this. I stopped at the Monoprix store on the rue de Rennes. The fridge was empty. Kamran was coming back and I could not continue to live on my reserves. I needed to feed myself, eat, drink, continue to exist even if this existence did not mean much since I had seen Sergei. I had the blues and my soul now only churned out blackness. I felt like a pebble being nudged forward by another pebble in the bed of a running stream. I was sinking. Reason told me to fill my fridge with food for my husband's return, but my body refused. I had to grab on to the escalator to not trip on it. I was shamed by the gaze of the security guard who usually saw me every two or three days. I was a regular. I was always cheerful, always saying, *'Bonjour,'* or, 'How are you today?' I liked these little rituals, these signs of respect which I had learned, first in my country, then in the United States, where informal contact with others – superficial as it may be – is easier than it is here. In just a few hours I had broken all my rules, gone beyond the landmarks I used to give me the illusion of a certain security.

It was cool inside the store. And in spite of all the appealing colours, gadgets, fabrics, different kinds of cosmetics, costume jewellery, everything that had made me a shopaholic the week before – now it felt as if I was entering a walk-in refrigerator. I took a shopping trolley, throwing things into it without thinking, grabbing things from each aisle at random. I would have it all delivered. I felt incapable of carrying anything, not even a bottle of water. For my dinner, I would put something in the microwave. I paid and walked down the stairs, my face hidden in my mass of hair, avoiding the security guard's eyes.

I got home around six o'clock and immediately began looking for that video, *Les Choses de la Vie*. Frenetically, room by room, rummaging through drawers and closets, lifting piles of files and books, emptying out my handbags, talking to myself. How stupid. But I could not stop. Did I want to immerse myself in the music, or the words? Probably both. The music, because it reminded me of the taxi, and the words because of the scene when Romy Schneider, playing a German translator, sits in front of her typewriter at dawn. Michel Piccoli and she have just made love. When she gets up she wraps herself in a blue towel, with her back to us, her hair up in a messy *chignon*, like the kind I sometimes make for myself with a pencil when I am hot or I need to concentrate. We see the bottom of her tanned neck, her soft skin. Suddenly she turns towards him, her face still consumed by passion.

She demands: 'What is the French word for "lie" – I mean, not lie, more "tell stories".'

'*Affabuler.*'

'That's it, *affabuler*!'

And he adds, with a tender smile: 'With two f's!'

I was looking for this cassette obsessively, neurotically, knowing I was deep into lying, not *affabulation* – when the telephone rang. It was Kamran. It could have been a telemarketer but I knew it was him. No one ever called me except him or my parents. In general, people would call my husband, then ask to speak to me, since we hang out with the same crowd, the same people. I answered, nervous and annoyed. 'You're so sweet, so calm,' Kamran would repeat. And it was true. Not any more. My evasive 'Hello?' collided with his sweet 'Roxane?' and suddenly I felt like sobbing or crying out, aware now of how much trouble I was in.

'Roxane, are you all right?'

'Sure.'

'Doesn't sound like it.'

'Yes yes, everything is fine. I just want you to come home. Oh, and I've been looking for that video everywhere.'

'What video?'

'The film, *Les Choses de la Vie* . . . I don't suppose you've seen it?'

'No.'

And he added: 'We've let ourselves be invaded a little too much of late, no? Don't worry about it, I'm sure you can get that film on DVD. I'll pick it up for you at the FNAC on Saturday.'

'Fine, sorry about that.'

'I kiss you.'

'I kiss you too.'

So I put away everything I had disturbed. Kamran likes order, as do I. We like what we call our 'lived-in mess'. And as long as there are books . . .

Early that evening I closed the curtains, lit some candles. And I thought about the things that unite us, and also about what separates us. Outside, the wind had risen, I could hear it whistling from my bed. I was exhausted and fell asleep whispering your name: 'Sergei.'

I woke up at dawn. In my head, chaos reigned. My thoughts were all jumbled together. I was no longer taking a sick day, I was going to have to figure out a way to coordinate my professional activities with the ones I thought of as illicit. I remembered we were going to be getting a large delivery of foreign novels at the bookshop. And these days were going to be difficult, because we had to do it all at the same time: sales, stocking the shelves, answering the phone. I needed to be on my game and not encourage any gossip. I took a very short shower, made myself a cup of strong, almost black tea, but had to pass on my scrambled eggs and toast, an Anglo-Saxon habit I had acquired. Knowing I would be going to the hospital in my lunch break, I dressed carefully, adding a few dabs of Shalimar, my favourite perfume. The idea that Sergei might be able to smell me, even if he could not see me, bothered me terribly. I imagined he probably didn't much like make-up and preferred loose hair with simple, unpretentious clothing. Kamran liked me to wear lipstick, dresses, sexy blouses. Glancing at myself for the last time in the hall mirror, I said to myself, laughing, that Sergei and Kamran had only one thing in common: a love of literature . . .

It took me perhaps ten minutes to walk to work. It was practical, and I was sometimes able to come home for lunch, which I much preferred. I went out with a single thought in my head, to appear to be the same woman I had been forty-eight hours earlier. No outward sign of my inner turmoil must show. I must appear calm and collected, not arousing the curiosity of others. I needed to appear to be someone I was not, or not any more: I needed to appear like a young woman whose life was not a novel.

At the bookshop they asked if I was feeling better, I said yes and everyone went back to work. In spite of my long list of things to do, I couldn't stop looking at the hands of the clock, waiting for my lunch break, and for you, Sergei. That morning I was lucky. My colleagues showed their usual lassitude and indifference towards each other, so I had no problem disappearing at lunchtime. I ran towards the No. 63 bus stop and caught the bus just as it was leaving. I had been gesturing the driver to wait for me as if my entire life depended on it, which in a way was true. As I stepped on to the bus, the driver smiled at me. I punched my ticket with lowered eyes, embarrassed, feeling confused.

The weather was uncertain: cloudy, then suddenly clear. It was cool, and the air felt good. A few metres away from the hospital, there was a florist. As I stood in front of the shop, breathing in the delicate scent of the multicoloured bunches of roses displayed in buckets on the pavement, I thought to myself how I would have liked to bring you flowers. But it was impossible, I could not leave a physical trace of my visits. So I thought about spiritual, invisible flowers. When I got to your room, I found you lying in exactly the same position, with the same expression on your face, peaceful, almost serene. In a very soft voice I recited to you this poem by Marceline Desbordes-Valmore which I know by heart:

> This morning I wanted to bring you roses;
> But I tried to hold so many in my tightly closed arms
> The too-tight knots could not hold them.
> The knots broke, the roses flew into the air,
> Into the wind, they flew to the sea.
> They followed the water, never to return.
> The waves turned red, swollen.
> This evening my dress is imbued with their scent . . .
> Breathe me, this fragrant memory.

I knew when I took your hand in mine – feeling your warmth and listening to your breathing – that you were no longer in danger. On your face I did not see bumps or shadows, you were a valley about to awaken in the coolness of the dawn.

So the week went by, and each day at lunchtime I came to sit by your bed. I would stay ten or fifteen minutes, no more. I would mentally sketch your face with great precision, then I would leave, sometimes serene, sometimes blitzed, lost. Because that was what concerned me, the danger of loss. Each evening Kamran called, and I told him I was fine. I slept and woke in sync with the rhythm of your nights. When I showered I ran the water for a long long time, over my face and my closed eyelids. I saw you everywhere. And I am sure that if you had been able to speak, you would have told me we were dreaming the same dreams, that I was thirsty when you were thirsty, hungry when you were hungry and afraid when you were afraid. The words beginning with 'tele' are not my favourites, but I looked up the exact definition of the word *telepathy* in the dictionary anyway: it means *the transmission of a thought from one person to another without using any of the known senses*. And I said to myself that if telepathy works, you would remember me, you'd remember the invisible roses I brought you.

And then I got the terrible news. You were better. It was Friday, around two o'clock, when I heard the diagnosis: you would be waking up soon. It was wonderful news. It was terrible.

I had just lost you.

TWO MONTHS LATER

> I turn the daily page,
> I write what is spoken
> By the movement of your lashes.
>
> Octavio Paz, Á travers

MY LIFE had gone back to normal. Nearly two months had passed since my last visit to the hospital. I had decided to drown myself in work and socialising. It was not at all like me. Kamran, rushing around between two scheduled trips abroad, was alarmed by the abrupt changes. He sounded me out, although perhaps that phrase is a little too strong for what he did. It might have been better if he had gone further. If he had become angry, if he'd made a scene, clearly expressed his doubts about the way I was acting, I would perhaps have listened and extinguished the fire which consumed me day and night. Paradoxically, his tenderness and understanding pushed me further towards betrayal. Kamran took on the wisdom of Asian women; like them, he was convinced that it was not through fear and authority that you hold on to love. To show affection, love and dependence is not a weakness in the Orient, it is more a sign of maturity and devotion for those who love us. Why not show one's feelings? Why try to appear hard and heartless? Kamran had chosen this softer manner of being, whereas I sought out possession and exclusivity. I needed a crash barrier. I needed him to hold me back, to raise his voice, just a little. To say to me, sharply: 'What's going on here, Roxane?' All the freedom he was giving me, which I had not used yet, made me dizzy. From my childhood days, my parents had put the 'apple of their eyes' in a finely wrought gold cage. I loved my prison and never felt closed in. I even missed it, having thought that Kamran would maintain the delicious system of house arrest they had established. He did so at the beginning of our exile, thinking he needed to protect me, but little by little he unburdened himself of the weight of this protection, leaving me alone and at a loose end more and more often.

I was anxious. I made myself a noisy presence in the house, slamming doors, letting my heels clip-clop across the wood floor, smashing dishes, turning music I hated up to blaring. I was irritated, tense, on edge. I wanted to go out every night, drink champagne, go to the cinema or to restaurants, go and see our friends. I talked and laughed too loudly. I became dependent, demanding, like I was at the beginning of our marriage. I insisted on going with Kamran on his business trips and had to ask for time off at the bookshop, which surprised my boss, who'd never seen me so skittish. Suddenly I wanted to go to London and New York, even though I already knew these cities quite well. My friends were getting tired of me, and I was tired of myself.

Then one Sunday, in the late morning, I gave in, saying to myself: 'Why fight? You want to see Sergei again? Well, go and look for him, go down that road as far as you can.' Running away and travelling the world was useless. It was a collision course, albeit a comfortable one – Kamran was always booked in at the best hotels, five stars, refined, historically or artistically important, and I liked that, but it was all useless. I was only 'elsewhere' in the geographical sense, since each particle of my body belonged to you. It was written that I would only be truly content under the weight of your gaze.

> Emotional exile
> Exiled from my country
> Exile from my emotions and from my home
> Three generations, three kinds of exile
> following each other.

When my parents are in Paris, we get together on Sundays, around a traditional Iranian lunch. Kamran would join us if he was available. It was a joyous time, like all those I spend with my family. My parents appreciated Kamran's company, asking his opinion of certain books, art exhibitions, films. They admired him and listened attentively to him. Even beyond their intellectual connection, my father and mother liked seeing Kamran and me together. They were comforted and reassured by the idea that their daughter was able to go beyond the melancholia engendered by memories of her privileged childhood, building something strong, rare and indestructible. I don't want them to question the connection I have to my husband. And if I do happen to say something sad or harsh about us as a couple, I feel bad, and the next day I erase the shadow of that bitterness, doubling my affection and my cheerfulness.

So this Sunday, Kamran called my parents from Milan, where he had had to stay over, apologising for not being there. He talked for a few minutes with my father, then my mother, then me, the usual. So as not to arouse the suspicion of my parents, I spoke very warmly. Only I heard the falsity of my voice, knew how unnatural I sounded, and how I was dying inside. Kamran was light years away from imagining what I was going through, what I was feeling.

After our meal, and after a card game in which I had to make sure I didn't make any obvious mistakes that would give away my inner turmoil, suddenly I realised what day it was. Sunday May 15th. This date seemed to be the anniversary of something. A voice buzzed inside my head, saying repeatedly, 'It's Sunday, it's Sunday.' I tried to make the voice go away, to concentrate on the card game. Feeling almost sick, I put down my cards, saying with a nervous laugh, 'I don't know what's the matter with me today, I'm playing so badly!' Then I got up and collected my coat and bag, ready to leave. For once I was going to leave them with their worries.

I wanted to retrace my steps, do an emotional reconstruction of the crime, although technically speaking, no crime was committed. There was just that one meeting. I did not know what effect a traumatic cranial injury would have, or what the consequences of a concussion were, if that is what had happened to Sergei. Would he want to sue someone, maybe the driver, or would he just want to forget what had happened? I hoped not. I mean, I did want him to forget the accident, but not me. I was walking towards the place Saint-Germain when the clouds suddenly covered up the last little bit of blue sky, and I could feel a storm brewing. I stopped in my tracks, wondering if this was a divine message, and whether I should listen.

In a few minutes, we would be in the middle of a rainy Sunday. The telephone would ring, and it would be Valarie inviting me to join her and her husband at the Brasserie Lipp. I would grab my raincoat, my bag and my silk scarf and run towards my destiny. 'Roxane, you're crazy,' I said to myself, looking up at the threatening black clouds. While everyone around me was hurrying, seeking shelter, there I stood as if nailed in place, waiting for the blessed rain, since it would reawaken my memories. A flash of lightning shook the trees in the place Saint-Germain, illuminating its deserted benches for a fraction of a second. And I said to myself: 'As long as it rains, I can imagine holding your hand in mine. Even afterwards, when the sky is wearing its softer colours, I will still be holding your hand.'

So I literally retraced my steps, stopping at the same places, reproducing with neurotic precision the scenes of that evening. Then, at the exact spot where I saw you fall, I lit the cigarette you never got to smoke. I looked for traces of blood on the asphalt, with a naivety which makes me smile in spite of myself. My pilgrimage included the café where you stopped to buy your two packs of cigarettes. I went inside. Aside from a couple of foreigners having a beer at the counter, there was no one there. Deciding to go for it, I asked the guy at the counter. 'A young man? An accident? When? A Sunday? Which Sunday?' No, he hadn't seen or heard anything. In any case, the café didn't have a clear angle on the quai . . . He asked one of his colleagues, who said she was not working on that Sunday and that waiters at the café changed constantly. I saw I was barking up the wrong tree, as it were. There were those who had seen something but who would say nothing, those who had seen nothing at all, and finally those who did not care one whit about things that did not directly involve them.

I went home, feeling lost.

I had recovered the clothing I was wearing on the evening of the accident, including the silk scarf I had placed on your wound. I still remembered what I had done, the softness of the improvised bandage. It was clean, too clean, and the sour smell of the dry-cleaning chemicals made me nauseous. For the first time in my life I cursed the talent of the dry-cleaner – it had stolen bits of you.

Then, in the following days, I changed my tactics.

My desire became sharper, clearer: focusing it had made it urgent. 'It is the magic of your gaze that is the base for the foundations of our souls,' wrote Hafez. Well, for mine, I needed Sergei's eyes, his blue eyes gazing straight into mine. Blue + grey = blue/grey. I needed this equation. At least once, just once. I told myself that if he was out of the hospital, he must have gone back to his regular life, which would not necessarily be built around a café, a bookshop, or a bakery. The passengers of my dreams, they used public transport, they travelled, they went to the cinema or to the theatre, they went out. So why not 'move around' like Sergei?

One evening, after work, on a whim, I took the Métro – or to be precise, I bought a *carnet* of ten tickets and began an underground journey to the places I thought I might run into my blue-eyed stranger. A passionate student of poetry will walk the streets, but he must also take the Métro, where he reads, observes, and hopes to meet people.

I started with the No. 4 line, of course, the one that cuts vertically through Paris towards the Porte d'Orléans and stops at many strategic stations: Châtelet, Cité, Saint-Michel, Odéon and Saint-Sulpice. It connects places that would be essential in the life of Sergei: his classes at the Sorbonne, his long solitary walks along the quais of the Seine, then hanging out with friends in the neighbouring cafés. I thought also about the No. 12 Line which stops at rue du Bac, Sèvres-Babylone, Rennes and Notre-Dame-des-Champs. The No. 1 Line goes to the Marais *quartier*, its gardens and its little courtyards, to the place des Vosges, the Picasso Museum, the Tuileries, the Louvre and the Pont-Neuf, so it might also be worthwhile. It was nearly eight o'clock and I was getting ready to go back to my flat, having tried perhaps ten stations, when suddenly my long quest came to an end at the Pont-Neuf station, where the barges are tied up along the banks of the Seine, and the booksellers' stalls line the quais. I was not mistaken. There he was, barrelling down the stairs, leaping into the Métro carriage just as the doors closed. I didn't even have time to look back down at my newspaper, which I held in my hand in case I got lucky and which I was using as a sort of screen against the unexpected. Of course, the unexpected was him. His eyes collided with mine. I was sitting on a fold-down seat at the back of the carriage, and was so taken aback by the sight of him that I tried to make myself as small as possible on my seat. This was the kind of encounter I'd been hoping for, but I was not prepared for it actually to happen. I was at a loss, trying to minimise, as always, the shock of stepping into reality. At the hospital the man I saw had his eyes closed, he was deathly pale and stretched out on his hospital bed. Here I was seeing a vibrant being, full of energy, looking like any other student of his age. He was wearing faded jeans and a grey sweater. He carried a black bag in one hand and in the other he held a thick book, probably a dictionary. He stared at me as if he recognised me. Unlike when we first met at the Brasserie Lipp – how free I felt when I first met his gaze – this time the emotion got to me and I dropped my eyes, suddenly full of doubts. Had he really recognised me or was he confusing me with someone else? Who or what was he remembering? I had given him so many Roxanes! Multiple versions; some of which would remain in the shadows for ever. Memory is such a cruel companion, debiting and crediting our memory accounts as it pleases.

Sergei, my Sergei. Perhaps his heart hesitated between the disobedient Roxane, the seductress, or the Roxane who came to his rescue? Did he have something to say about the Roxane in the taxi or about the Roxane from the restaurant, who at the time had seemed so daring? And if he could only keep one of these Roxanes, which one would he choose? I wished I could find the state I was in the first time my eyes met his. I could taste the kisses he had not yet given me and which I was already stealing from him, while rambling on about the thousand nuances of blue and taking small sips of the sweet white wine, which reminded me of Iran. Yes, I would have let down my guard, I would have thrown out a few words as one might send a bottle out to sea. Just to hear the sound of his voice and to savour the music of his accent mixed with my own.

But that evening, fate only allowed us this short space of silence inside the screeching Métro carriage, which bounced us back and forth against the soulless metal rails and doors instead of bringing us closer together.

We stayed like that, him standing, leaning on the back of the banquette, and I, numb with emotion, sitting on my little *strapontin,* until the next station. What would he do at Châtelet? Would I find out one day?

When he got off, I was prepared to speak to him, and I think he wanted to say something to me, but the sound of the doors closing sent us crashing back to our states of muteness. Watching him as he drew farther and farther away on the quai, I already burned with impatience at the idea of seeing him again. I knew it, Sergei and I definitely had a *rendezvous*. In this life, not in any other.

'Roxane! Ro–xane!'

'Yes?'

'Are you ready?'

'Ready? For what?'

Kamran opened his eyes, astonished.

'The theatre. We're seeing a ballet this evening.'

'At the theatre?'

'Yes, at the Théâtre de la Ville. I reserved the tickets a long time ago, it's that new piece by Pina Bausch that you wanted so much to see . . . '

'Oh, right. Yes.'

He looked at my messy hair, my casual attire, my pale lips mirroring my earlier distress, which were definitely not obeying my long-standing 'smile no matter what' rule.

'Are you ill? If you don't feel well, we'll just stay at home.'

'No, no way. I'll go and put on a dress, it'll take me five minutes.'

Normally, it would indeed have taken me only five minutes. It is crazy what I can accomplish in just five minutes: pack a suitcase, reserve plane tickets, pay our bills, make shopping lists. Kamran likes how I multi-task in record time. So normally, I would have run and picked out a dress at random and fixed my hair, but I was lost. I was still sitting in that Métro, with the blueness of his gaze piercing my soul.

Kamran was never cross. Not with me, at least. Our friends and his closest colleagues often spoke of his perfectionism, his severity, his inflexibility at work. But I did not know that man. The man I lived with only brought home books, manuscripts, maybe a few files, but never his problems. We spoke freely about our doubts, our fears, our regrets, but all these feelings originated in our roots, our sadness that we could not buy a plane ticket to Tehran in the same way as you would to London or Berlin.

In the car, I asked myself this question: are we all like this, doubled? Do we all have two faces? One that we show, the other which we keep hidden, answerable to our moods, our failures, our betrayals. This freedom we claim to have is nothing more than a reassuring opiate, to help us move forward, to renounce our dangerous desire to die.

At the theatre, I opened the programme an usher had given me, and read: 'As always in the creations of Pina Bausch, love is the eternal object of our desire, we cannot give it up. To do so would be to deprive us of all hope, of the meaning of life.' And then, farther on, 'The road leading to love is rarely easy.' Was this a cliché or an overwhelming truth?

Kamran, as he often did when we went to the theatre or to an art opening, ran into some of his friends. So I had to be there for the after-performance ritual, the usual drink at a late-night bar. I went along with them. Listening to the others telling each other their stories, congratulating each other – allowed me to escape back to my Métro carriage at the Pont-Neuf station. Kamran was chattering enough for two, all I had to do was nod my head from time to time and smile at the appropriate moment.

We went to bed very late. The next day, when I finally emerged from a troubled sleep, he had already left for the office. On the kitchen table I found a bag of still-warm croissants, and a note: 'Don't wait for me for dinner, I'll be back late. Don't stay too late at the bookshop, I thought you looked very pale last night. I love you. Would you like to come with me to Turin next week? Kamran.'

And once again I resented him for offering me my freedom that morning, without a second thought. Millimetre by millimetre he was pushing me towards my lie – without realising it, of course. He was even giving me ideas on how I could use him, use the time he was giving me. After all, he had a dinner, he would be back late.

I wasn't hungry. I drank some coffee and got dressed. Carefully. As soon as I walked out of my building, I knew I was going to my *rendezvous*, I was already on my way.

At the bookshop I was a little less cheerful than usual, as well as less interested. I wondered if I still liked my job, if I still loved anything or anyone – aside from Sergei. I had become like the others, counting the hours of the day, waiting for my break. A few more days and I would be checking off holidays on the calendar. That day, I walked towards the No. 63 bus stop, then sat down on a bench in the place Saint-Germain to eat a sandwich. The afternoon went on and on, I couldn't hide my boredom. I had plenty of work stacking up, but I just didn't feel up to it. That evening, towards seven o'clock, I took a walk over to the rue Jacob, then wandered along the quais. It was rather nice out and the Seine was cloaked in the slate-grey colour which evokes a certain melancholia. A light, cooling breeze ruffled my hair as I walked. Then I saw him, a few metres away. He was walking quickly, as if he were late for something. I speeded up, wanting to narrow the distance between us. I could feel my heart thumping in my chest. I was paralysed, yet ready for anything. Suddenly, he turned around. Had he felt a presence behind him or was he waiting for me? He smiled – his disarming, spontaneous smile – and I froze. With the Seine in the background, against the changing sky, he looked a little like a tourist dazzled by the sun, posing for a holiday snap. In a few seconds I was going to hear the sound of his voice for the first time. I saw that this time he was going to step across the line of our mutual shyness – and speak. He approached me, and spoke these first words, which will for ever be engraved in our memories – words which were entirely banal, yet unique in the force of meaning we gave them.

'You live in Paris?' he asked me, looking me in the eye.

Abashed, I hesitated a few seconds before answering. So he had seen it all, understood it all, grasped it all. He was calling me 'tu' and already knew I was not from France. And his voice – his voice was clear, cool, with a pronounced accent, not easily identifiable.

'Yes, I live here,' I said, pulling nervously at the strap of my handbag.

If he didn't go on, immediately, I would die or have to run away, because I would never be able to separate the images of our common past and those of right now. I could not escape the idea that I had something he didn't know about, the secret of his accident. At the same time we needed to go forward, towards what I had been building, starting that memorable evening at the Brasserie Lipp.

'Are you taking the Métro at Pont-Neuf or at Châtelet?' he asked, as if he understood how hard it was for me to speak.

I would take the Métro wherever he wanted; I would follow him to the ends of the world, on foot, on a bus, on the Métro. I had already been following him for a long time in my thoughts. But how could I tell him this without appearing to be giving myself to him already, body and soul? He was still staring at me and the blue of his eyes still overwhelmed me. I don't know how or why we suddenly decided. Somehow our eyes must have exchanged some sort of signal. Neither of us had chosen to walk in any particular direction but there we were, standing in front of the Pont-Neuf Métro station. I was clumsy, mute, awkward, I had not said a single word although my body was on fire. I could not stop looking at his hands, the hands I had caressed at the hospital, which I so longed to clutch to my breast. At that instant I realised I would never, ever forget him. The magnetism of his body, of his being, had shaken me from my head to my feet, with the strength of an earthquake, a typhoon.

'Would you like to have a coffee or a tea with me one of these days?'

'Yes,' I managed to say, relieved that he was not discouraged by my apparent inability to speak.

He understood. He understood me.

'Tomorrow, in the place Saint-Germain, around one o'clock?'

'Tomorrow, yes.'

So his memory was working, he remembered the place Saint-Germain, and the game of hide-and-seek we had played from the boulevard Saint-Germain to the Saint-Germain church, then to the quai Malaquais. That was good.

'I think I'll walk home,' I decided, all of a sudden, seeking to be spared, for at least a few hours, the heat of his gaze.

He stared at me intently. For a second I thought he had recognised me as the person who had come to his rescue, that the coma had perhaps not affected him, but I discounted the idea immediately. We waved at each other and then separated, walking in opposite directions.

It took me at least fifteen minutes to pull myself together. I was overwhelmed. In spite of his placid appearance I was sure that he too had been shaken by our meeting. Had he suffered any after-effects of his accident, and if so, how? He appeared rested, calm, no one would have thought he was convalescing. 'When you're young, you recover faster,' I said to myself as I arrived in front of my building. I thought suddenly of his age, twenty-six as of last 13 January, according to his student ID, and of mine, thirty-five . . .

At around 8.30 p.m., just after the news, I decided I would not be going to the rendezvous. I did not want to be one of those 'older women who seduce younger men'. Then at 9 p.m. I decided I might as well go, 'just to see'. At 10 p.m. I changed my mind again, and at midnight, after I had taken a light sleeping pill, I postponed my decision until the next morning.

For once I awoke before Kamran. I had heard him come home late that night, but I didn't move when he tiptoed in to give me a furtive kiss on my bare shoulder. I shivered a little inside, happy, yet guilty, glad to be escaping an embrace which would have broken my heart. I thought obsessively about Sergei's hands. It seemed that those hands had been designed specially for me, made to hold me, to caress me, to take me. Their strength and their fragility had marked me so deeply I could have drawn them from memory. During my uneven sleep, I considered what I would wear, the words I would say. I scared myself, too, with a rising wave of 'what ifs': 'What if my boss won't let me take my break?' 'What if Sergei doesn't come?' 'What if Kamran invites me to go to lunch with him?' I managed to brush all of these hypotheses away, except for the most important one: 'What if he doesn't find me attractive?'

After stealing access to so many of his private moments, I was already ahead in the game. Would he hold it against me that I watched over him at the hospital? No, because he would never know. Never. No one likes to be watched while they are sleeping. And what did he know about me? Nothing. However, when he asked if I lived in Paris, he showed his perspicacity. He had guessed I was a foreigner, like him – that was perhaps my one good quality in his eyes.

After a thousand hesitations, while Kamran was beginning to move around in our bedroom, I picked out a pair of black pants and a colourful blouse with geometric patterns. I had bought it in Milan on a whim and had never worn it. In a few hours, these garments would belong to Sergei for eternity. I liked this idea of a visual 'gift' to him. I realised that Kamran would soon be coming into the kitchen; from the bathroom I heard him turning on the radio as he did every morning. I needed to leave before he did. I could not see him, look at him. I could not deal with having to answer: 'No, I can't,' if he invited me to come with him to Turin. Leaving the apartment in such a hurry, I was for the first time skipping our morning ritual of having coffee together, something we had always done.

'Kamran!' I called, 'I don't have time to have breakfast with you, but I've made your coffee, and there's fresh-squeezed orange juice and scrambled eggs, it's all on the table.'

I did not hear his answer.

Would Sergei be there? I could not stop asking myself this painful question the whole morning. Happily my colleagues didn't leave me time to think about anything but work. We had had some problems with an order from England, and I worked on it all morning. I decided that being a little late wouldn't be a bad thing, it would suggest a certain nonchalance and help me overcome my fear. I would apologise for having made him wait and the conversation would begin by itself. Alas, that was not my nature. I could never be late. Being extremely punctual is a symptom of exile. We want to be everywhere, even if one day we are told we belong nowhere.

There is no reason to plan, to over-organise, to anticipate events; the most interesting are those which evade our control. We arrived at the exact same time at the place Saint-Germain. Perfect synchronisation. So perfect it did not seem real.

'I'm Sergei,' he said warmly, extending his hand. 'How are you?'

I smiled.

'Hello, Sergei.'

He suggested we walk a little and we turned towards the rue Bonaparte, in the opposite direction from our first walk. It was strange, yet exciting, to be together in this laid-back new context after having gone through such difficult times before. I let myself follow Sergei's cheerful spontaneity. His childlike attitude both pleased and intrigued me. He was both man and child as I was both woman and child. The difference in our ages brought us together instead of pushing us apart, and our physical differences complemented each other. His blond brightness contrasted with my olive skin, my dark hair and eyes. I glanced at the windows of the antique shops we were passing, and what I saw there made me feel more vulnerable, ever closer to the lie I was still trying to deny. Together we were light and shadow, and the sensation was infinitely troubling. I felt so close to him, I realised I would reveal the story of my entire life to him in a second, and I wouldn't be surprised if he said he knew everything about me. We walked side by side, already inside each other, our souls fusing, communicating with secret signals that only we could identify.

For once it was not me who decided. Clearly Sergei knew where he wanted to take me. I walked, rather I floated next to him, feeling like I was gliding on a velvet carpet. The street was narrow and noisy, buses, bicycles and cars passing each other with inches to spare. We could not speak, but that was fine, the silence protected the secrets and the whispers which were to come.

Sergei knew my neighbourhood better than I did. He stopped in front of an entrance way and firmly pushed the door open. I stepped into one of those wonderful interior courtyards which make Paris so mysterious. At the back of the courtyard a red sign announced the presence of a *salon de thé*. A Russian tea house, Sergei told me. He came here very often, preferring this quaint, quiet place to the many loud bistros in the area. Seeing the cracked façade and the rather baroque entrance, I thought about the café in the rue Jacob where I had begun my initial investigation into Sergei's habits. How far off I was. This out-of-the-ordinary place was removed from the hustle and bustle of Paris – it fitted us perfectly. From now on we would have 'our' place. As he walked in front of me, leading me as was the custom, I almost revealed everything, but then thought better of it. We did not have time for the truth, not for this truth. After all, I couldn't be more than half an hour late for the bookshop.

I drank my first Russian tea on a wobbly wooden table, painted red like the walls of the *salon*. That day we talked about everything and anything except our lives. This frantic discussion allowed us to confirm what we already knew: we belonged to each other; it was one of those divine laws that cannot be rationalised. Each time one of us said something, the other would exclaim, 'Me too!' We asked each other questions, we marvelled, we skipped all commas, all punctuation, as if it was essential to condense everything, as if in the background there was the threat of a new exile, a new separation. As if we feared saying goodbye. A breath of freedom wafted through our words, relieving us of the weight of convention, formality. A spontaneous trust had been established between us, even if I was constantly censoring myself, afraid I might reveal what had seemingly been forgotten.

Like me, always and even now, he stumbled over certain

letters, had trouble with certain sounds, the right French word for certain emotions; we switched to English, as one might pass from one continent to another without having to show our passports. We spoke of the difficulties of French grammar, its pitfalls – and he glanced briefly at my gold wedding ring which shone a little too much in the subdued lighting. He did not look in the least surprised. 'There will be many more meetings,' I tried convincing myself, but felt an inexplicable sadness. Time was passing so quickly. I was supposed to be back at the bookshop and he – ? To class probably, or something else. We said goodbye quickly, with great reserve, facing each other, staring at each other, standing in the entrance way, which would for ever be the location of our forbidden games. There also, our two cultures converged. When physical contact is complicated, it is necessary to invent other codes, find other meanings which carry messages and protect secrets. I think he said: 'Here, tomorrow, same time?' And I smiled.

My detachment spoke for me as I pushed open the door of the bookshop. How could I go back to the world of the living when I had spent more than an hour drinking Russian tea with such an inspiring and wonderful man? The response came very quickly. For the first time in years, I received a chilly reception at the shop. The staff told me I was being egotistical, inconsistent, unreliable, unprofessional and indifferent to anyone else's problems. Ouch. I did not argue. Deep down, I knew they were right. I accepted their uncompromising judgement. I had changed. And this change, imperceptible at the beginning, had become palpable, visible to those around me. There was only Kamran, maintaining his careful blindness. He was linear, predictable, and I would be lying if I said this did not please me, but my meeting with Sergei had opened a new stream into the depths of my soul. Without knowing it, he had pushed me to explore different perspectives, to place my own interests in danger, when normally all my instincts steered me towards stability. No, I couldn't fault my colleagues for chastising me for being late, for saying all those disagreeable things. They were right. But whatever they said, whatever they did, I could not go back.

'I don't understand people who live double lives, how do they do it?' my friend Valarie asked one day, intrigued. 'You're right, I couldn't do it,' I replied with conviction. And it was true, I couldn't. And yet somehow I had slid into a parallel life, and I didn't know how I came to be there. Every day I saw Sergei, and every day I lied to Kamran with the assurance of someone who has done it all her life. I lied, cheated, told foolish, even ridiculous stories in order to escape our social life, our daily life. Sometimes I exaggerated things greatly on purpose, to test my limits – and his. And this brilliant, intelligent, kind man believed me. He accepted my excuses and my miserable evasions without blinking. Sometimes I would stumble, unable to face his generous, loving gaze, hoping he would ask me the one question which would trip me up and make me confess all. My eyes watered, my throat was tight. But his questions were not in the least devious. He did not understand how devastating his questions were. He was straightforward, simple: 'Roxane, are you all right? Are you sure?' he asked, with annoying concern. I sighed, and he thought I was perhaps just tired, when really I was expressing my lassitude and self-loathing.

I lied to my parents, to our friends, even when I didn't need to. I anticipated my lies, presenting them on a silver tray wherever I went, running on autopilot. I felt the endless chaos of a world in which we disappear into our own stories, indifferent to anyone else's. I was sinking, drifting, and no one saw it. I was also now refusing point-blank to leave Paris, even for a couple of days. For me there was no difference between going to Normandy for the weekend, two hundred kilometres from Paris, and going to the end of the world. I was mixing things up, dramatising every second away from Sergei.

Of course I was having intense, pure moments with him, but in the evening I paid heavily for all the minutes I spent immersed in his blue eyes and absorbed in his words. And his kisses. His furtive, chaste kisses, stolen when the people around us were not looking. He had not yet invited me to come to his apartment. He showed self-restraint, as well as his fear that he might disappoint me by a gesture or a word betraying his eagerness or his passion. He was not in a hurry. I felt a sharpening of my senses, increasing tenfold my desire for him.

Like teenagers, we would note our meetings on little pieces of paper, write with a felt-tip pen on the insides of our hands or on the tab of a pack of cigarettes. We almost always met at the Russian tea *salon*, or, weather permitting, at the Luxembourg Garden, at the Tuileries, somewhere along the quais of the Seine. He spoke to me with great naivety, reading me the poems of Pushkin. His masculine yet delicate voice captivated me. He liked it when I in turn recited Persian poetry to him. 'So, you're Iranian?' he asked me, astonished, without asking me for more details. All we needed was to know that we were both exiles looking for a new life, far from our roots.

The night before each meeting we would choose the passages we would read the next day. And for that I also had to hide, to lie. I would wait for Kamran to fall asleep, then look carefully for photos, stories, ballads, quatrains, drawings or lithographs that Sergei might find interesting. I would delicately mark certain pages, sticking Post-its here and there, underlining some lines in pencil, and I loved it. All these words and images kept me connected to him twenty-four hours a day. We were linked together by the magic of this luminous secret, burning continuously in our souls.

    I had bought the famous collection of the poems of Pablo Neruda, which Sergei had had in his pocket the day of the accident. Without thinking and without being in the least discreet, I had put the book into my bag with the DVD of *Les Choses de la Vie*, which Kamran had thoughtfully bought for me. The temptation to play the music for him, the symbol of our first encounter, haunted me day and night. This torment followed me even to work, where I continued on autopilot. I watched the minutes passing on the wall clock. I wanted to make him happy, I wanted him to think of me at my prettiest, I wanted him to keep me in his pocket like one of his favourite books. He had listened to me attentively, with great tenderness, when I told him about my idea of life as a painting which is never finished. I applied myself to painting a small piece of that painting for him, for later, when we would say goodbye, because I did not doubt that this moment would come – and sooner than I wanted.

One day he gave me an anthology of Russian poetry. The next day I brought him a bilingual edition, in English and French, of the mystical poems of Rumi. Sergei already understood both English and Spanish.

I was waiting for the moment when he would mention our meeting at the brasserie, the accident and what he might have remembered afterwards. But it had been too abrupt, too violent. How could he have seen the white car that hit him, then me, running to save him, and then the taxi . . . I was waiting for him to talk about himself, his life, his exile. I didn't want to precipitate anything. We needed to calm ourselves, to lower the heat on the fascination we had felt upon discovering each other, so alike, so close.

He began to open up, finally, one rainy afternoon

when we kept pushing back the time for us to separate. I was sitting at the tea *salon*, but he was ten minutes late, something which had never happened. I had of course imagined everything under the sun, including the possibility of another accident. Or maybe he had simply grown tired of our meetings, perhaps he would not be coming any more?

Each new minute that passed confirmed my fears. I stared fixedly at the door and each time it opened I stopped breathing. I hated everyone who came through that door who was not Sergei. No, he wasn't coming. He couldn't wait any longer for our bodies to connect, to discover each other. But was I really ready to give myself to him entirely, and to hate myself for the rest of my life? While I was asking myself this terrible question, he appeared in the doorway, clearly out of breath. I was shaking so much I almost began to cry. He saw my distress and ran to our table, taking my hands in his.

'I am so sorry, my Spanish professor started his class late.'

I could barely speak. He began covering my cheeks with little kisses and I had to close my eyes, feeling his joy at being with me.

'I thought that – '

'No, no, I would never do that to you, you have become so important in my life.'

Finally I pulled myself together, and he sat down across from me without releasing my hands, clutching them so hard he was almost crushing them.

'I am ridiculous,' I stammered.

'No, not at all, but you must believe in me,' he said gravely.

At that instant, I thought he might bring up the circumstances of his accident, but I was wrong, because he began speaking rapidly – and for the first time – about his life in Russia. Sergei came from Novgorod, a village near St Petersburg. The oldest son of a family of six children, of modest origins, he had been awarded a grant to study applied languages at the university and had taken a small room near the Neva. He was enthusiastic about his studies and spent most of his time in the library, surrounded by the Spanish culture he liked so much. Students and teachers, Russians and foreigners met each other at the campus cafeteria, a space overflowing with curious minds thirsty for knowledge. There, full of joyful exuberance, he would argue for hours about politics, art and literature. And like other young men his age, he dreamed of the world beyond, of freedom, but what he saw around him undermined his hopes significantly.

One morning when he was having a cup of coffee, standing at the bar of the cafeteria, he glimpsed a cloud of golden curls, then a small hand, filling pages and pages with rapid writing. He was fascinated by this luminous beauty in such a smoky, dilapidated place. He gazed at her long enough for her to lift her graceful eyes from her work. And a few seconds later the young woman's face was revealed. She was a little older than him. Pen in hand, she smiled at him, a soft, dreamy smile. There was something indefinable in her manner that encouraged him to approach her table. He felt instinctively that she was a foreigner but he spoke to her in Russian.

'Hello, excuse my impertinence. I've been watching you for a while and I've been wondering what you're doing. Are you working on an interesting project?'

'My name is Maya,' she said, delighted, in perfect Russian. 'I was rewriting for the gazillionth time the introduction to my class, because today I'm teaching my first French class at this university.'

'My name is Sergei,' he replied, touched by her directness.

She was only a little older than the students she would be teaching, and was clearly suffering from stage fright. Suddenly Sergei felt he should protect her, or at least reassure her.

'Don't worry, your students are going to be inspired by you.'

'You think so?'

She blushed, and Sergei felt he had been too clumsy. Instead of reassuring her, maybe he had made her more uneasy. He saw her looking in panic at her watch. She quickly put her notebook away in the briefcase she had left on a nearby chair.

'I have to go now,' she said.

'It will be fine, I'm sure of it,' he told her.

He did not, however, dare to ask if she would like him to go with her to her class. But he did add, in a joking tone: 'At least I know where to find you in the early morning!'

She giggled without saying anything, appearing less anxious now, and Sergei felt much better. They separated at the entrance to the building where classes in the French, English and Spanish languages were given. For the next few days they met at the cafeteria. The young woman was French, from Paris, and she was three years older than him. Soon they became intimate, in secret, since personal relationships between students and teachers were frowned on by the university. In reality, Maya was much less timid and fragile than she had appeared that first morning. She knew exactly what she wanted. She was clever and fearless, making big plans for the future. She was also pragmatic, organising everything, finding ways around the obstacles that separated them. She would ask friends in Paris to send Sergei books in French and Spanish, as there was nothing similar in St Petersburg and they were far too expensive in Russia. Maya earned enough to live on but it was out of the question for Sergei to accept any help from her. He even insisted on paying for all the books he had received from France.

Little by little, as Sergei told me his story, I put together the pieces of the puzzle. So the young blonde woman the barman of the rue Jacob had mentioned – was her, Maya. What came next I had already guessed, but I let Sergei tell his story all the way to the end. Maya loved him deeply, she wanted to help him, somehow to give him wings to discover the world, to escape the Russia which no longer inspired him. Sergei liked Maya very much, admiring her courage, tenacity, and strength. He appreciated her company, the time they spent together. He liked making love to her and could not resist her charm and her exalted sensuality. But he was not in love with her. After several months of their relationship, harmonious and satisfying for Maya, but incomplete and ambiguous for Sergei, she offered to marry him and take him back to France with her.

Summer vacation was coming. Maya could not reasonably extend for much longer her stay in St Petersburg: for her this had been no more than a pleasant year abroad, and she needed to get back to finish her degree. After thinking about it for a long time and discussing it with his parents, who showed a rare altruism in encouraging their oldest son to leave, he accepted her offer. The choice was a cruel one, cause for regret and eternal remorse: should he stay in Russia and give up his dreams, or accept a marriage of convenience which might bring him a taste of freedom? He decided to believe Maya, she who was promising him everything he had hoped for. So they married, but they were not happy and they did not live happily ever after.

In Paris, everything was different. Sergei discovered both France and Parisian life. At first the experience was a euphoric one, since his lack of money meant he had never travelled, even in his own country. Maya went back to her friends, to her job at the university, and they lived in her little two-room apartment in the rue Jacob. The apartment was not big enough for a young, independent couple and it quickly became the theatre of their conflicts. They could not even study together without fighting. Finally they worked out a schedule which would give each of them a certain amount of time alone in the apartment to work. And this way they only met in passing. Maya was no longer the exotic woman who had seduced him in St Petersburg. She had become distant, withdrawn, coming home late at night or sometimes not at all. Sometimes she stayed with friends or went off for the weekend without him. As for Sergei, he was taken aback by this new life which had so little in common with the one he had imagined. He enrolled at the Sorbonne and began looking for translation work to earn his living. Unexpectedly he did rather well, working on and off with several publishers, and soon he was able to pay his half of the rent, his tuition and even a few dinners out at a restaurant. He imagined himself in a couple of years teaching, like Maya, but not at the university, perhaps at a high school or a middle school. He sometimes missed his family and his country to an extent that he considered going back to St Petersburg. He wrote to them regularly, telling them everything was going well and that he was happy. And he would attempt to convince himself that this was true, telling himself he could build something new, far from his native land. Reading a good book, attending a good lecture, seeing an interesting exhibition or taking a late-night stroll along the Seine were enough to restore his confidence, in spite of the misunderstandings and tensions which continued between him and Maya. Every day the situation got worse, to the point where they decided to separate, each to go his or her own way. A friend of Maya's had introduced Sergei to a young English teacher looking for flatmates to share a large apartment in Montparnasse. He was planning to move there next month.

At this point in the story, Sergei stopped and looked deeply into my eyes, wincing a little. He had been speaking for more than an hour. Several times the waitress had signalled to us that the tea *salon* was closing. As 'regulars' we were entitled to a few privileges, staying an extra ten minutes after the last customer had left and having 'our' table always reserved for us. It was after seven o'clock and we really did have to leave. As I was putting on my coat, Sergei said: 'You also are married, yes?'

'Yes.'

'And exiled?'

'Yes.'

'But not from your marriage.'

My heart sank and I murmured with an uncertain voice: 'No. No, I guess not.'

'I understand.'

He continued in a thoughtful voice: 'I don't know what is happening, but – it's strange, I have the feeling I've known you for a long time, that I have seen you somewhere before. I'm intrigued . . . '

Distressed, I dropped my eyes, incapable of answering. Outside I felt a cool breeze on my face. I was not in a hurry to go home. Once more, Kamran had gone away without me. Far away, this time. He was in Japan, looking for – and finding – foreign publishers to whom he could sell book rights. I had been tempted to go with him, as the chance to discover that country would not come up again for a long time – but I didn't go. So I could invite Sergei to my home. Nothing was stopping me. He asked if he could walk me home, and I knew his respect for me would prevent him from asking for more than a chaste kiss on the cheek as we stood at my door. An exile's feeling of emptiness never goes away, but sometimes, with patience and courage, one can heal the wounds, or transcend them and find strength instead of weakness in them.

That night I wrote him several letters, which I immediately tore up. In one of them, the longest, I told him everything. I told him I could no longer stay silent, pretending to be a stranger to him when in truth I had been privy to an important piece of his life. I did not want to be a burden to him, an extra complication in his daily life, I wanted to protect him, to push him to live fully the courageous experiment which he had begun, so far from home, which he needed to finish, against all odds. I told him also that I loved him to the point where I would even accept in silence the possibility of sharing him with Maya, should his relationship with her change for the better. And, of course, as I wrote this I was thinking about my life and my relationship with Kamran. I wrote to him late into the night, but then, deciding all this had taken a far too moralistic tone, I got rid of the letters, witnesses to my turmoil.

Sergei wasn't someone who complained a lot. He had the rare talent of being able to relativise, to reach out and catch in flight even the smallest pleasure that came his way. His capacity to create a sense of happiness attracted me like a magnet. When a cloud disturbed the pure blue of his eyes it would bother me, too. One day, when we were walking along the quais by the Seine, I found him very pensive, almost absent. After a moment, I asked: 'What's the matter with you today? Has anything happened?'

He didn't answer right away. Then he stared at me with such intensity that my heart began to race. In his eyes I found love – but also something else, a mute interrogation, perhaps. He began talking about his accident. He remembered having been hit by a car. He spoke slowly, looking for the words, and I could see he was racking his memory for answers. I don't know how I managed to stay calm, his gaze was so compelling. I could not look away. I had the impression he was searching for an answer.

'I think it was a woman who saved me,' he said suddenly.

'Oh . . . and did you see her, this woman?' I asked, trying to sound as natural as possible.

'No. No, I didn't see her. It all happened so fast. I was coming out of a restaurant where I had been with some friends . . . I remember the *bar tabac* where I got my cigarettes. After that I don't remember, it's all so vague. I know only that I was very lucky. Apparently I hit my head very hard on the pavement, but the doctors said the oedema was absorbed very quickly.'

'Ah.'

I let him continue. He obviously needed to talk and seemed relieved to be getting this stuff off his chest.

'You know, Roxane, it is difficult to live knowing you owe your life to someone you can never thank.'

'Yes. I understand, of course. And – what are you planning to do to find this person?'

'I went back to A & E.'

'Really?' I said, dumbfounded.

'But they didn't know anything. One of the paramedics thought it was a taxi driver who brought me in, but he wasn't sure.'

'Well, the most important thing is that you're healthy now, right?'

'Yes, of course.'

'And your wife, I mean Maya, she must have been worried?'

'Yes, although not right away. She was off visiting her parents in the country for a few days. So when she got back she looked for me. She called our mutual friends, then she went to the police and the hospitals. And she found me, but – '

'But?'

He grabbed me and held me close, whispering: 'It's strange, crazy even – but I think that the woman who saved me is the woman I will love for ever.'

As time went by, he continued to search for his 'mystery woman'. I didn't see him doing anything specific but I knew it was on his mind. Perhaps he thought that chance or destiny would one day bring him the key to this unknown chapter. We did not speak any more about the accident. We were beginning to lose control of our kisses. The physical attraction we felt for each other was overwhelming. I was thinking less and less about controlling my impulses or making them go away. The very foundation of my education was more or less going up in flames, but I could not escape the desire which obsessed both of us. I had even begun saying to myself that it would be better to suffer because I had betrayed someone than to suffer for nothing. One evening it became clear that we were focused on the same thing: a hotel room, curtains we could close, a bed for our entwined bodies. I had never made love in this way, and nor had Sergei. It was this ignorance, this naivety which allowed us to transcend the tackiness, the sordid nature of our situation. We were not looking for five-star hotels, prestigious façades, fancy gilt decorations, acres of red velvet. We wanted to drink our passion down to the dregs. The stars were shining in our souls, and we were counting on their luminance to enable us somehow to escape the divine punishment of forbidden lovers. We tossed a coin to choose between Saint-Germain-des-Prés, Montparnasse or Saint-Michel. Heads it would be him pushing open the door, tails it would be me. Heads he would decide, tails it would be me. Secretly, shamefully, I hoped that he would have to choose, because I might then escape the terrible guilt which would soon devour my soul. *Tails*. No, I was not being spared by fate. I was in, all the way.

I was lying naked, my head buried in the pillow, the sheet pulled up to my eyes. Sergei had slid in beside me without a word. I could feel the heat of his body, his heart pounding, we were a thousand beats jumbled together. I had seen him undressing in the shadows, his eyes cast down. Our fears and our modesty spoke to each other, accepting each other unconditionally. His body was as I had imagined it at the hospital, through the thin sheet that covered him. His muscular form and the softness of his pale torso made me want to take him in my arms. He had smiled at me from far away, as if he wanted to record the features of my face somewhere in his memory, which he could have lost for ever on that evening in March. He looked for some music on the radio built into the television cabinet. Then he came towards the bed, where I had suddenly taken refuge in a blind panic. I did not know this was going to be so difficult.

'I want you so much,' he whispered, pulling me further into his embrace.

'Me too,' I answered, as my burning throat closed off so that I could only sob mutely.

He began caressing my body with the very tips of his fingers, with a delicateness that dazzled and terrified my senses. My muscles were beyond tense, and my confused thoughts brought me brutally back to my dilemma. I had dreamed of this moment from our very first meeting, but somehow an unknown force held me back from the intense attraction. 'Without him, life would be unbearable,' a little voice whispered as I was fighting to keep control of this sensual moment, which I desired and rejected at the same time. After tonight – if I spent the night with him – I would be lost. My life was elsewhere, far from all these lies, and closer, much closer to renunciation that I had expected. I needed to get up, pull away from this inescapable embrace, and leave. 'No, I can't,' I begged myself, hoping he would not hear my prayer, because that is what it was, a prayer. He sat up and looked at me, surprised.

'You aren't sure any more?' he asked. In his eyes I saw his distress.

'I can't,' I said in a slightly louder voice, trying not to be affected by how upset he looked, his still-warm lips, the softness of his skin.

It was over. Everything that had bonded us over the last few weeks passed in front of my eyes; I was already beginning to see specific excerpts, my own *Choses de la Vie*, from a distance, as if I didn't know the principal players. But in the emotion of the moment I caught my breath, tears forming in my burning eyes. I knew what was going to happen, and I knew it would take superhuman strength ever to find inner peace again. I also knew that the tiniest hope of that peace would be extinguished if I made love to Sergei. My life was elsewhere, on the other side of the door of this hotel room, these windows, and it was waiting for me. I do not know where I found the strength to get dressed, there in front of him, as he lay naked and handsome on the bed. His angelic eyes were shining. As I walked towards the bathroom, I heard him get out of bed too.

'Wait, don't move,' he said, grabbing me by the shoulder. 'Don't turn around.'

I felt him writing something on my back. I laughed nervously, wanting to stop him, but he begged me to stay still. He said: 'I want to write to you in secret.'

Apart from the completely bizarre nature of the situation, I was again tempted to forget the words I had spoken. I loved Sergei's skin, his smell, his warmth – my determination was wavering.

'OK,' he said in a satisfied voice. 'Now I have told you everything with these words which I have written in Russian. They come from the bottom of my heart and tell you everything you need to know, since you have decided to leave.'

'Do you want to read them to me?' I asked, intrigued.

'No, you know that the written word has a power which words read aloud do not.'

'So what can I do? Who will read them to me?'

I was trying to joke, but I was dangerously close to tears.

'I'll have to undress; do you know a Russian doctor?'

He laughed, but neither of us was fooled.

'Will you hold me?' I said.

He drew me to him, held me, rocking me gently like a child. I began to cry, soundlessly, my head in the hollow of his shoulder.

When I left, when I fled the hotel room, I was closing the door on passion. I did not want to leave, but I had no other choice. An irresistible force was pushing me to leave.

The next day, I emerged nauseated from a short, agitated sleep. I called the bookshop and told my boss that I was sick, in the literal sense of the word. I could not get out of bed, it seemed to be pitching wildly, like a boat on a stormy sea. Cold sweat was running down my back, my cheeks were burning, and I felt a stabbing pain at my temples. I crept into the kitchen. I could barely stand. I made myself a little tea and then staggered back to bed. The violence of my physical reaction did not surprise me. I remembered that when I was a child, I would keep quiet about any great sadness, until my body, exhausted, gave in to the dark forces preying upon it. I would develop a cold, a stomach ache, a migraine, even a skin rash, and my parents were at a loss. And then, a few days later it would be gone, my body would be back to normal and all would be well with the world.

I stayed in bed for the whole day, wrapped in my quilt, my eyes glued to the telephone, which I clutched in my hand.

It was ridiculous. I knew Sergei would not call, for the simple reason that he did not have my number. He had given me his number, which I had written in pencil on the title page of one of my favourite books. I did not put his name in the book. I forbade myself to dial the number. What if Maya answered? Sergei had said it was all over between them, but should I believe him? There were so many questions and unspoken stories between us, underlying our story. Sergei did not know my last name, just my address. I knew he would not come to my house without letting me know beforehand. He was much too respectful to come and ring my doorbell, turning up without knowing if my husband was at home or not. I was on fire, then I was cold, then hot, then shivering again. My belly cried out for food but I couldn't risk swallowing anything. I drank a little water and slept a few hours. I thought about Kamran. He had not called either. And I would have liked to hear his voice. This urgent need to speak to him was paradoxical, but I accepted it. I was alone. Alone in my turmoil. No one could help me. I had made my choice, and no matter how painful it was, I needed to accept the consequences.

Suddenly, towards the middle of the afternoon, as I continued to battle my dark thoughts, I remembered Sergei's goodbye present. Forgetting my headache and my lingering nausea, I got up, terrified by the idea that it might have rubbed off or evaporated. I ran into the bathroom and tore off the three sweaters I had put on when I was shivering. I grabbed a magnifying mirror and stood with my back to the wall mirror, trying to decipher the letters of a language whose alphabet I could not read. These few words were all that I had left of Sergei. I sighed in relief. I could not read the words, but at least I had not rubbed them off in my sleep. I got dressed again with extreme caution and found myself staring at my own reflection. My face was smooth, my skin clear, my complexion luminous, as if someone had smoothed it out. My feverish eyes were those of a woman in love, a happy woman. And yet, I was also a broken woman, torn up inside – the memory of all those happy moments was stronger than the pain I suffered today. Did the pain of our separation affect me so little after all?

I was back in the living room looking over our immense library of books. There were so many of them – albums, anthologies, fiction, sorted by author and alphabetised – but no Russian dictionary.

After thinking a little, I decided to go out. If I wanted to find a solution to my problem I had to stop hiding in my apartment. I needed to walk, to force myself to take a Métro or a bus. I would go where chance took me, somewhere I might find someone I could trust enough be able to undress in front of him or her. Before going out I sat down and made myself eat a little.

I had one hand ready to close my front door, in the

other I held my keys, but for some reason I hesitated. Should I really go out? Why? Again I felt the need to roll up in a ball, to remain at home with my sadness. Playing tourist in the streets of Paris, wandering along the quais, inhaling the smells of the night, talking for hours about the colour of the sky, about a poem that had moved us – moments like this had been wonderful with Sergei. With him I had wings, I felt invincible. But without him I was too small, fragile, incapable of facing what was to come. Discouraged, I retraced my steps and collapsed on the couch in the living room. I was now obsessed with the words I carried in me, on me, against me. I needed to find help. But it was not in my nature to seek it out. In fact, to my knowledge, I had never asked anyone for help. 'Roxane, you must learn that you can count only on yourself,' my father would say. I had learned that lesson and had usually applied it, but today my pride was of no importance. I started mechanically flipping through our address book and realised quickly that every single name and number listed was linked somehow to Kamran.

I was on my own.

I put the address book down on the coffee table and lay back on the couch, my hands crossed on my chest, as if to muffle the beating of my heart. Suddenly I saw a face, neither Sergei's or Kamran's – it was the face of an older man with sad eyes. His lips seemed to be saying something to me. I sat up abruptly, transfixed by what I had just remembered. It had happened perhaps three months ago, on a weekday. At the bookshop, I had quarrelled a little with one of my colleagues when we were closing. I was tired of the argument and tired of her. Kamran was out of town, so I was in no hurry to get home. I decided I should maybe walk off the tension of the day. I walked a little way, then jumped on the No. 63 bus just as its doors were closing. I stamped my ticket and went to sit in the back of the bus. The bus was full but not too full, surprising for a weekday at this time of the evening. Sitting next to me was an old man reading a slim book, perhaps poetry or short stories. I was intrigued. I stole a glance at it, looking for the title – it's a professional reflex, I always do that when I see someone absorbed in a book, no matter what it is, just to know what others are reading – but I was too close and I couldn't see anything. So instead I examined the man reading it, looking at his elegant profile. He wore round horn-rimmed glasses which would slide down his nose each time the bus swerved or braked. He would calmly push them back up and continue reading with an amazing serenity. We passed several bus stops before he lifted his head, seemingly as settled in on the bus as one might be in a doctor's waiting room.

After a while, consumed with curiosity and, in truth, wanting to speak to someone, I asked: 'Monsieur, excuse my intrusion, but are you sure you have not missed your stop?'

He took off his glasses and turned to me, smiling. His gaze was that of a man who has suffered, but who has also learned to forgive. His direct, unequivocal gaze was reassuring.

'I am not going anywhere in particular,' he said in a detached voice.

'Oh, really?'

Suddenly I was ashamed. This man was clearly just looking for a little peace and quiet on the bus, and here I was interrupting him with my stupid question. I was going to excuse myself, but he continued, in a friendlier voice.

'I work at a linguistic research centre, my office is at République, on the other side of town. I think I have already tried all the bus routes in Paris.'

I laughed, amused by the originality of his idea, knowing that I would also be capable of doing something just like that. His manner had intrigued me, and then his kindness had made me feel a little less as though I were intruding.

'What languages are studied at your centre?'

'I write and speak eleven different languages,' he said modestly. 'But I specialise in Slavic languages, particularly the Russian language. I am fascinated by Russia and its history and I have done a great deal of research on the Bolshevik revolution. I was born in Armenia, and I learned Armenian as a child.'

He stopped, looking at me carefully.

'You – you're a child of the sun, yes?'

The phrasing of the question made me laugh.

'You might say that! I am Iranian, born in 1979 in Tehran. My family left Iran at the time of the revolution.'

He had just pressed the 'next stop' button. He was still staring at me, and I think my little-girl-lost air touched him somehow.

'Here's my card. If ever I can be of help to you, call me,' he said graciously, even paternally.

I smiled at him. Comforted by the delight of our little exchange, I accepted his card and tucked it away in my diary, without imagining the vital importance it would have so many months later. As he walked around a street corner, he waved at me. I waved back. I got off at the next stop, feeling like I was floating on a cloud.

While I was wandering through that waking dream, which had surprised me at the lowest point of my desperation, I had not thought to look at the telephone. But there was the little red light blinking, telling me I had a message. It was Kamran, of course. His voice flowed into me like honey, even though my entire being was vibrating in silence, calling out for a different voice, and for a specific colour: blue. But I wanted to heal, and I needed to forget that blue, its nuances and its unending depth – which had stolen me away. Kamran was the man with whom I shared everything. He was for me the earth of Iran, the perfume of the Persian gardens, the architecture and the light of the city of my birth. And I loved Sergei with a love that knew no time limits. I loved the intensity of our shared moment, its fleeting nature. He would have children one day, with Maya or with someone else. Not with me. He would travel, study, trying always to go beyond his limits and to sublimate the pain of exile. His life would be filled with love, with cool water and unexpected moments of pleasure. Like my life had been, yesterday.

But here we are today. After the rain comes the fine weather, they say . . . I want to believe that after suffering like this, the light will come back, the eclipse will last only as long as the time it would take me to count down to – you, you who will carry me so gently towards the shore, to that strip of dry land, far from the blue of your eyes, there where that essential truth still waits for me. I would love to understand what goes through the heads of those who decide to go away, to leave everything behind in order to forget. What drives them? Is leaving a sign of power or of weakness?

The next day I woke up early, feeling rather cheerful given the fragility of my emotional state. I was still wavering, asking myself whether I should leave or stay, rather like being on a ship and not knowing which way to turn the rudder. The problem of choice, now and for ever. Could I walk away without any 'baggage'? Could I leave behind the words, the taxi, the music, the night and the stars, the smell of his skin and his own scent, the silk scarf we both wore that rainy night, the restaurant menus, the mirrors, the streets – could I walk straight up to the ticket counter at the airport, carrying nothing, my hands in my pockets? I would have only my soul, heavy with fears and doubts: 'The real travellers are those who leave for leaving's sake,' wrote Baudelaire. Would I be able to do that? And if I could, where would I go? It seemed that the far countries were crying out my name, preparing for me the transformation of a love which had been condemned from the beginning. Not long ago, I tossed a coin to pick a hotel. Now I would open my diary to the map of the world and I would put my finger down somewhere at random. And then –

Before leaving for good, or leaving in order to flee, I wanted to test my capacity to transform a question mark into a full-stop. I wanted to contact the man I had met on the bus, who had so kindly and spontaneously offered me his help. I would take his outstretched hand, and I would know. Someone was going to tell me the truth about what Sergei had thought and then written.

When I took my shower that morning I looked at myself for a long time in the mirror. Normally I let myself go, stepping heedlessly into the full force of the water, my eyes closed, my hands open. But today my eyes were open, and I was careful how I manipulated the shower head, holding my breath so as not to erase Sergei's words. I could get the words off easily if I rubbed them with a flannel and some soap or a strong make-up remover. But I had decided to keep the words, to protect them. I had categorically refused the ephemeral, yet I was fighting so hard to forget. Oh, none of this makes any sense, but that is where I was, at least at that moment. If I could grasp the significance of the message, it would perhaps be one way of turning the page, cutting short the fantasies. Because I was programmed for an honest life. To refuse it now would be to refuse myself, my roots.

It was a little after nine o'clock when I dialled the number of the old professor. I did not know who would answer, nor how to introduce myself. After three rings, a female voice answered: 'Yes?'

'Hello, I'd like to speak to the professor.'

'The professor is busy right now. Can you tell me what it is in connection with?'

'It's personal,' I replied curtly.

'Just a minute, please.'

I waited for an eternity. The woman had put me on hold. Realising I might be late for the bookshop, I was about to hang up when she came back on the line.

'Sorry for the wait, but things are really busy this morning. Could you call back in an hour?'

'No!' I was even more abrupt. I continued, 'It's because I have to leave, I really do need to speak to him now. Could you tell him that we met on the No. 63 bus, a few months ago?'

I could hear her sighing. This time she wasn't so careful with the phone. Ouch. I waited, my heart pounding.

'Yes?' he said, in a deep voice I would have recognised anywhere. It was him.

'Hello, professor. I don't know if you remember me, but – '

'Yes, the No. 63 bus, I remember perfectly. What can I do for you?'

'Well, er – '

'Yes?'

His voice was warm, but I could tell he was in a hurry. And he was going to think I was crazy, but I realised I had nothing left to lose.

'May I come to see you at your office?'

'Oh! Of course, why not.'

I continued in a slightly embarrassed voice: 'I know my request is a little strange, but you did give me your card, so I thought – '

'Fine. I'll wait for you here, shall we say at seven o'clock this evening?'

'Perfect! Thank you so much.'

'You're welcome. So – see you later.'

And I hung up, relieved. My request must have intrigued him, or must have seemed incongruous, but I was counting on his intelligence and his perceptiveness, sure he would understand my emotional turmoil and my rather unique predicament.

I was back at work at the bookshop, everything had gone back to normal. My colleagues no longer looked at me strangely. We all did our work, staying in our respective parts of the shop, just as we had done before. Every time I recommended a book or stepped into the foreign-literature section, I thought of Sergei. What am I saying? I thought of him all the time, even when I wasn't busy. I remembered our discussions, our kisses, the tea *salon*. Then I remembered the hotel room and that big bed I never wanted to leave. I remembered all of it, all the while trying to set little goals for myself. I needed to resist the temptation to wander over to the rue Jacob or to drink Russian tea. I needed to read something besides poetry, to discover new restaurants. I would not take another taxi and I would love all colours except blue. The list was long and I certainly had enough imagination to make it longer. And all the while I thought about the words written on my back, this sentence I carried like a second skin. What had he written? 'I love you', or, 'I cannot live without you', 'Stay with me', 'Don't forget me'. As soon as the professor had translated the words, I would rub them off. Immediately, without thinking about it. If I thought about it I would fall again, drown again, and I so wanted to swim, peacefully, in a calm sea. I wanted to climb back inside my painting, as if I were going home, with the certainty that all would be pardoned, that I would be loved and cherished no matter what.

I took the Métro to the République station. The professor's office was at 118, rue du Temple. At seven o'clock on the dot I walked up the stairs. Fourth floor, the door facing the lift. I rang the bell. He opened the door. His kind smile told me I was wrong to have worried about my action. Everything in him spoke to me with understanding and compassion. I told him some of my story. He listened attentively. Finally the moment came when I would have to show him my back, my body. Oddly, although I had always felt shy and uncomfortable when I had had to undress for a doctor, I found myself perfectly at ease as

I unbuttoned my blouse. This man could have been my father. I uncovered my back where Sergei had written his message. The professor drew closer, looking at me in a detached, clinical fashion, and I understood he was putting me at ease, acting as if he was merely translating a simple document. He said, softly: ' "I know it is you." '

'You – Are you sure?' I asked, in shock.

He nodded. 'Sure.'

I continued, stubbornly: 'Maybe some of the letters were erased. The water, perhaps my clothing – '

'No, I am sure, this is what it says. I understand if you would like to ask someone else to look at it.'

'No, no, I'm sorry. I believe you, I do. It's just that – '

'You didn't expect this.'

'No.'

'What else can I do for you?'

'Nothing. I – I need to get some air.'

I could not fall apart or burst into tears in front of this man. I needed to be alone, free to cry out, to fall on my knees in pain if I felt like it. I thanked the professor in a near whisper, then made my way out of his office. The lift was occupied, so I decided to take the stairs, but nearly tripped over a loose corner of carpet. My legs were suddenly heavy, weighed down by my sadness, my grief. *'I know it is you.'* The words tore open the sky above me like a bolt of lightning. I found myself standing in the dark on the rue du Temple, in a neighbourhood I did not know and which seemed somewhat hostile. It was raining, as it was that March evening when our eyes had met for the first time. My eyes filled with tears as I crossed the place de la République and I went down into the first Métro entrance I saw. So. Sergei knew my secret. He had guessed what I had tried so desperately to hide from him. He knew, but perhaps he did not know what I knew? Perhaps he thought that after I left the hotel I would not try to have his message translated, that I would erase it in order to forget?

He would never know how this last revelation had moved me. And I would never know exactly when he had understood what I had been burning to tell him. We had both lived with our secrets, our hypotheses, our silent questions to which we would never have answers.

After all the tears, after the rain, far from the tumult of our hearts and of the sadnesses of exile, there is a place where better things await you, me, us. It is a star in the sky, the sound of an angel, an eclipse of the moon, or a colour fading all the way to infinity.

It is you.